praise for

so my mother,
she lives in the clouds

"The stories in this wonderful debut collection, told with both heart and imagination, spin the broken and the beautiful together to create a world we can all recognize."
  - Sequoia Nagamatsu, Managing Editor at *Psychopomp Magazine*

"...tangible yet ephemeral."
  - Patricia Colleen Murphy, Founding Editor of *Superstition Review*

"There's something free in the urgency of DiCicco's imaginative prose ... a vulnerable and honest innocence rooted in the complex doubt of our lives."
  - Paul Elwork, author of *The Girl Who Would Speak for the Dead*

"Sweet...strange...feels like a late-night conversation, relationship-sticky and dreamily half-whispered."
                  - Leesa Cross-Smith, Editor at *WhiskeyPaper*

"There is a lonesome magic to the characters inhabiting *So My Mother, She Lives in the Clouds*, their longings so red-hot they manifest in fantastic, haunting ways."
          - Justin Lawrence Daugherty, Managing Editor at *Sundog Lit*

so my mother,
she lives in the clouds

and other stories

christopher d. dicicco

HYPERTROPHIC PRESS

For Anna,

for my father,
for his father too,
for all fathers and sons
who write their hearts out
for one reason or another.

contents

TALK OF FIRE

I've got an impulse. It's real bad. And it's getting worse.

I don't want to die. I just want to burn for a little to show that I can. I imagine flames, being engulfed in them, me sitting down in my small desk chair.

Except.

I want people everywhere to watch me. I want my professor to look at me and get lost in my hot orange glow. I want my classmates to bear witness. I want everyone to. I want them to see me burn and I want them to see me talk.

I want to talk to them. On fire.

I want my burning mouth to open up like there is nothing wrong with what is going on in the world, the room, with me. I want my words to come out crackling, like they're consuming the oxygen we need.

It's not a protest. There're monks for that. I just want to burn for forty-five minutes. One lecture period. And my friend Jimmy says he'll help me.

He says he can't make it so I'll burn for a full forty-five

minutes, but maybe forty seconds. That should give me enough time to walk into class, sit down, and say "I'm ready to learn."

We layer me up in the bathroom, using clothes drenched in cold water. It's crucial that these go on first, Jimmy tells me. I shiver and choke and find it hard to breathe. The cold is something I hate. It slows down the heart, making it hurt.

I just want to warm the world.

The last two layers Jimmy helps me with are as crisp as an autumn leaf. The sweatshirt reeks of gasoline and Jimmy explains how he soaked it and let it dry for a week.

"Good," I say.

Outside the door to the lecture hall, Jimmy takes out the lighter and makes sure I'm covered from head to toe one more time. Only the bottom half of my face is left to the elements so I can say what I have to say. He sparks the lighter as a test. That quick flash reminds me of the importance of being seen.

Then it's time for me to open the door, and I do, and I burn.

I burn and I hear the words. They sound just like I thought they would – like crackling flame consuming everything I have to say to the world.

so my mother,
   she lives in the clouds

SO MY MOTHER,
SHE LIVES IN THE CLOUDS

The thing about my father is he tells stories you wouldn't believe. He says "Simon, did you know there are dragons in these woods?" I have to shake my head because I don't, because it's necessary to admit I have no idea dragons live here if I want him to keep telling his story.

And I do.

I want the story.

"Do you see this?" he says, pointing at what looks like a dead vine wrapped around a tree. "Dragon tail. Don't touch it. Burns the skin, leaves a painful rash."

I nod my head.

"Where's the dragon?" I ask, studying the furry brown vine traveling up the trunk.

My father points to the top of the massive oak. "You can't see him. He blends in with the clouds."

"Like a chameleon?" I ask. We've been learning about them in school. Ms. Kriggle says it's real magic what chameleons can do.

"Yeah, camouflage. He looks like the sky," my father says. "You can't see him, but he's there."

"Where?" I ask.

"On top of the tree," my father says, "the very top. He's perched there like a gigantic bird."

"All day?" I ask.

"All day," my father says, "eating clouds as they float by."

"And you're sure he's up there? Right now, on this tree?" I ask, attempting to touch the vine my father says is a tail.

"Don't do that," he says, stopping my hand. "Remember about the tail."

I let it go, touching the vine, and instead imagine a dragon the color of the sky staring down at me.

"Dad, are you sure? Because you said something like that about Mom, and now Ms. Kriggle is really upset with me."

"She's not upset. Don't worry. Ms. Kriggle's just a little confused is all," my father says.

He puts his arm around my shoulders, stares at the top of the tree, up beyond the clouds, a little farther even.

He's looking for her.

Except I don't believe Mom's there, not like how he tells it. I don't believe that story. Or the one about the dragon.

"It's okay if there's not one," I say, looking at the clouds circling the top of the tree. My father, he doesn't say anything. Instead he takes off his gloves and scratches his hands like crazy.

"I hate wearing these things," he says, motioning to the coarse workman's gloves he lets fall to the ground. "They drive me insane."

I smile and try to imagine he's not.

"What would it look like to see a cloud swallowed by a dragon you can't even see?" I ask him.

"The cloud you're looking at, it just disappears," says my father.

"And how many clouds do they have to eat to live?"

"Eighteen a day. That's enough."

"Eighteen? Really? That's enough for a dragon to live on?"

"No," my father says, "it's enough to get them where they need to go."

"Where's that?" I ask.

My father becomes sad, stares at his feet before lifting his head to look at the clouds. "To where your mom is. They go there. And if you time it right, you can catch a ride."

"Dad?"

"Sometimes, your mom told me, if the dragon's in a good mood, he'll take you with him. But cloud dragons, she said, are unpredictable and hard to control – even for her, a cloud princess."

In the sky, clouds float.

I look to see if any disappear, swallowed by dragons, but can't be sure if what I see is what my mind wants or what my heart needs.

"Are you going to be in trouble?" I ask my father, and I mean it, too. I'm worried. When I told Ms. Kriggle my mother went to live in the clouds, she wanted to know why I'd think that, so I told her I didn't really, that the story was just so nice, so wonderful, I couldn't help it, even if I knew it wasn't true. "It's just a really good story," I said to Ms. Kriggle when she cried and asked about my mom. "It's just a little better than thinking she packed up and left." Ms.

Kriggle, she covered her face when I told her. She shook big shakes full of sad, and that's why I worried – because Ms. Kriggle, she wants to speak to my dad.

She doesn't believe him either.

Inside the classroom, my father waits for the last of us to filter out the door. He waits for Ms. Kriggle to stack paper. He waits in a child's chair. And the funny thing, the thing about my father, is he fits in it. Though the chair is meant for a child, he fits right in without a struggle. My father, he's not a big guy. He's soft, small, handsome. Different. The kind of guy, he says, who a princess falls in love with, but wouldn't sacrifice her kingdom for.

He tells her, my teacher, Ms. Kriggle, he's sorry, he shouldn't have told me that story. Ms. Kriggle says, "I'm glad you understand, Mr. Rulik, but it's not Simon I'm worried about. He seems to understand it's only a story, a story he likes. I mean, Mr. Rulik, he likes your story, but I'm kind of wondering why you're telling it, if maybe you aren't yourself still having trouble processing what happened to your wife. And God knows, I'm sorry. I'm not sure of the details. I don't even know what happened, Mr. Rulik, but maybe you should talk with someone. I mean, I'll never understand what you're going through. I'm sorry. Don't cry. I just want to say it's a good story, Mr. Rulik. And if you ever need to talk or maybe want me to keep an eye out for Simon – anything at all – I'm here."

"It's a good story, isn't it?" my father asks. His voice cracks, and when he says it, I imagine what he looks like on the other side of the door, seated across from Ms. Kriggle. I see his shoulders, the heaviness there, the heaving up and down, his breath slow, face wrinkled, eyes sad.

I can see him.

And it makes me want a story.

The thing about my father is he doesn't wear gloves outside when he should. I can tell because his hands itch like crazy. They're red from not listening to his own advice. He takes the vine again, pulls, even when I ask him to stop. "Dad, it's okay. Really, it's alright."

He pulls again.

"Remember what Mom said, Dad: They're unpredictable, right? You can't control these things. You can't even see them."

He's crying now, pulling harder, more often.

"Dad, stop. Stop it."

He wraps some of the furry brown ivy vine around his wrist, yanks it, kicks the tree. "Come down here!" he yells. "We want to see her!"

He calls for the princess. He yells for my mom. "Sara!" he roars at the tree.

He pulls the vine harder.

"Goddamn it! Take us to her!" he shouts. "She's in the clouds, you stupid fucking beast! Come down, please!"

I reach my hand out, put it on his shoulder.

"Dad," I say, "stop. C'mon, please."

On the ground, his gloves rest.

I reach down, pick them up.

"Dad, the tail – it's poison. You said so yourself," I say, handing him his gloves.

He ignores the advice, the gloves too, and tugs a small, sad pull on the vine.

And then it happens.

When I grab his coat and say "I love you. Stop. C'mon, she's not up there, Dad. She's not," the thing happens. The thing about my father and his stories, it happens.

He pulls again, and the sky, it just kind of falls, just like that – clouds, blue, crashing down on us. And when it hits, it's heavy like an entire school building landing, like a father telling his son she's gone. It lands so hard we fall, the both of us, to the ground and stare at the fallen sky in front of us spreading its wings. Cloud patches ripple across the chest. And when we finally stand, my father, he looks from his red hands to me and says, "Remember about the tail."

WELL, THIS IS CHANGE

When I fall into a well, it's like a hundred-pound bird plummeting from the sky. When I'm at the bottom, nearly dead, I imagine my fall is something more like a hundred-pound feather falling from a bird's wing instead – slow and heavy, taking its time to get to the ground.

I fall into wells whenever I get bored or there's a commercial on TV. At least it seems that way to my family. Aunt Sal, she's all I have – unless you consider all the change at the bottom of the well to be mine. If you do, I'm probably richer than the boy next door. Jon-Jon, his family's huge and they love strangers, especially me because I'm poor and dirty like them, but hungrier.

I don't stay long, eat a peanut butter sandwich on discount bread, let his mom give me an old *Appetite for Destruction* T-shirt Jon's father forgot to take, and I'm gone.

Where to? To one of those wells I always seem to find in nowhere Pennsylvania, down away from everyone awful, away from where townies act like everything is fine.

There's no illusion at the bottom of a well, so I go for peace of mind.

Because there's change there, not like how it is everywhere else.

At the bottom of a well, things make more sense.

Quarters.

Pennies.

Dimes and nickels.

They're there, but no one looks for them. No one wishes for penny dreams. Not anymore.

Except, when I'm down there, the community remembers. They dream of healthy sons, their daughters smiling, last vacations where everything seems prettier.

And, at the bottom, when I'm there, Aunt Sal yells, "You down in that well? Simon? You okay?"

It's like she really cares when she cries.

It echoes, and to me it sounds like a hundred people calling down to see if I'm alright.

"Just broken," I yell for her to hear, for all those people caring about me.

They come with their ladders, their sirens. They cry, hold me to their chests, pull me out. Me. Not anything else.

The firemen, they don't even fill up their pockets.

At the bottom of a well, I remind the public about what really matters. Nickels, dimes, dreams, life – people have to choose what's important. But lately I've been sitting in the dark longer and longer, surrounded by rainwater and stone.

Lately, I'm afraid no one's coming.

I'd been down there two days before an employee from a Marcellus Shale company heard me singing and dragged me out. He used some rope under the arms, didn't even tell his boss, gave me the crust off his sandwich, told me to get lost.

In black grime, in hunger, I knocked on my neighbor Jon-Jon's screen door. It was a light rapping, but for anyone who owns a ripped screen door attached to a tin trailer, the sound of destitute knocking is a familiar one. It's something like a broken air conditioner and a plastic bottle of tequila your mom drops before falling asleep. It's not a bad sound once you get used to it. It beats the sound of my aunt – the sound of nothing at all and empty pantry doors.

My neighbor, he stood there in front of me, said, "Come on in, you're letting the AC out."

We both laughed at his joke, but stopped quick.

"I've got to tell you something," I said. "I'm going away for a while, so I'll see you never, then after maybe soon."

Jon-Jon knew what I meant.

I wasn't coming back. No one was looking. And really, he wasn't going to tell. Not this time. It wasn't his fault. Why should he? Things just become less and less important as your clothes get dirtier and dirtier, your stomach hungrier and hungrier.

It's hard to care. It's hard to really feel anything at all.

At least at the bottom of a well I knew how valuable I was. I could count the change.

Poor Jon-Jon.

I hugged him, started in about how his family were the best neighbors I'd ever had except for the nickels and dimes down below.

Nothing kept me company like the change people threw away.

Before I left, I said very serious-like, "Jon-Jon, I fall into wells like it's what I live for. I drop down without blinking an eye."

He stared, looked like he might cry.

"And if you listen to my splash," I said to him, "I swear to you, Jon-Jon, it sounds the same as a well-wisher's change clanging, dreaming of something better."

He laughed, swore I must be made of nickels and dimes, said, "The other boys say you probably sound like pennies cause that's all anyone throws nowadays."

I laughed with him.

"Is that how much our wishes are worth?" I asked before leaving.

No wonder they never come true.

But me, I've been saving up. I'm gonna get what I want even if it breaks my bones and pierces a lung.

When they hoist me up and blood's coming from where my teeth should be, I'll smile, say, "Hey, how was it up here while I was gone?"

It's only when they pull me free, hospitalize and bandage me, when they toss me back to her, that I kick, that I cry, that I wish.

If only I had a thousand quarters, a million ways out.

They throw me back, down into my aunt's house. And Aunt Sal, she doesn't care like she should. She searches my pockets for leftover meds, smacks my ribs, yells, "You won't give 'em? I'll make you wish you'd swallowed them all."

But it's only pennies she finds.

Not enough change to make her stop, so she breaks the mirror, chases me with a shard, tires and ties the rubber around her arm, asks me to help make it tight.

As soon as she's gone, I'm off, looking for a field with a hole to who knows where. Because the farther down I find myself, the more I think I'm worth.

LIFE WHERE YOU WANT IT

When I'm at work spinning in my useless rolly chair, sometimes I stop, stare into the cubicle across from me, and wonder about the woman who used to sit there, about whether she's upside down or in Vegas ripping pages out of books, watching pages turn to birds, watching birds turn to butterflies.

Those are things I think about when I think of her – upside down.

That woman, the woman I used to work with, she obsessed over roller coasters. It was the stupidest thing. Or at least I thought it was until she explained how sometimes when you're on a roller coaster, the kind that do all the loops, they stop it – or better yet, it gets stuck – right when you're upside down.

She sat in my chair when she told me the story. She put her hands on her knees and spun herself around in quick, tight circles to emphasize her point – that I had no idea what it really meant to be upside down.

When she stopped spinning, she stared at the wall with her back to me. She said, "You don't get what it looks like to see the world the way you want it."

I nodded because at the time I could only think right-side up. I had no idea what the possibilities were.

"Once," she said, "I was stuck that way on a roller coaster for forty-five minutes and I imagined a world where everything was really strange and wonderful, like really different, you know? Everything."

She spun around in my chair a few more times, stared around the office like she was somewhere else, somewhere fantastic, a place removed from our cubicle walls.

She said, "Upside down on that roller coaster my mother still loved my dad. When they pointed up at me stuck there, suspended in the loop, well, to my eyes, it looked like my mother grabbed onto him, and my dad, he finally wrapped his arm around her waist like he loved her."

The woman who used to work in a cubicle as small as mine, she smiled and said, "That's not all, though."

I nodded my head, thinking of fathers holding mothers underneath daughters stuck high above them. I wondered what else changed upside down. I thought about what could be different, felt confused and shook my head.

"Can you imagine?" she asked.

I couldn't, so I agreed to go along the next time she went and hope for a malfunction or an operator who knew what the people on his ride wanted.

And afterward, what I know now, is that when they stop the roller coaster, when they leave you upside down, your thoughts first go to your possessions. You get scared your material prizes will fall into the hands of the people below, that the people below will now go around wearing your Prada sunglasses, that they will make away with your wallet, that you'll have no proof as to who you are.

After that, you stop thinking about those things because those things seem silly when you're upside down. Instead, your mind wanders to survival.

What if I don't make it down? What if I were to fall out of my harness? Those thoughts bring about more introspective ones, ones that ask what you might do differently before you die. Then even those thoughts fade and you're left to imagine what life would be like if everything were upside down.

What life would be like if you didn't walk in to work tomorrow.

If you rode in on a horse and work was a castle in Scotland.

Or maybe it's a bike and you're called Crusher and everyone likes you and the stories you tell.

Upside down you wonder what life would be if you didn't say hi to the woman who stands in front of you every day getting coffee. If you mouthed *I love you* and kissed her and she dropped her coffee, letting it spill on the floor, becoming a lake that the two of you sail across when you want to be alone.

Upside down, you imagine what life would be like if the tundra were warm and the polar bears ate only honey.

You imagine what life would be like if all the people below you, underneath the roller coaster, standing, staring straight up, waving their arms and pointing, what if they always cared whether you lived or died?

After a while, it happens – you stop thinking right-side up. You stop thinking about what if or how come, about cubicle walls being relative to mazes. You start to consider things you didn't think were possible – raindrops hitting the earth, drying it up; closing your eyes to be awake; walking down to your basement to step into your attic – a whole mess of possibilities so extreme and weird that the realization of getting stuck in a daily loop, of spinning around in your cubicle chair for the rest of your life, doesn't seem so odd, so hard to believe.

HEAVY SHOES

My girlfriend imagines butterflies. She pictures little pain-ted wings falling to the ground, beating against the cement, unable to fly. They're failed attempts, she says, weak tries at propelling their bodies up after their disappearing souls.

"Their tiny, winged spirits float away," Sara says, "and they never come back."

"What? That's terrible," I say, trying to imagine what it'd be like to watch my own soul float away from my body.

Sara tells me it's like sprinkling rose petals across a wet bathroom floor on Valentine's Day – the rose is now ruined. Pieces of a whole. Torn. And she explains that, like the rose, this is sad because the butterflies aren't dead, they're only dying.

"Death is fine," Sara says. "It's the dying part that's terrible, the part where you begin to float away, but your body stays behind, a dead weight left for everyone to stare at."

She can tell I'm sick of hearing her say this, but she

believes it, my girlfriend Sara, and she wears heavy shoes.

Sara owns a horse back at her parents' house, or at least she did. The horse belongs to her little brother Ivan now, but when it's sick, he calls asking what to do.

And my girlfriend, it's always the same with her, no matter how slight the injury.

Take him out to pasture, she tells him. He's suffering.

Sara's left foot is wider than her right by half an inch, making it hard to buy her shoes. But that hasn't been a problem lately because my girlfriend, Sara, she's been afraid to take her Dr. Martens off for almost an entire year.

She says, "They're the only thing keeping me from floating away."

She doesn't want me to leave. Sara loves me too much. She says it, too.

"I love you like a thousand-pound boulder," she says. "You keep me grounded."

"What does that even mean?" I ask, and we both laugh.

But honestly, it's over. I can't risk being with someone who's only with me because she wears boots that weigh more than my hands, maybe more than my hands holding my heart.

I can't gamble on that.

Because what if someone were to untie Sara's Docs while we're eating dinner? A forkful of spaghetti and – POOF. She's gone.

There goes the wedding plans.

How would I tell my parents that their dream of watching us walk down the aisle floated away between mouthfuls of ACME brand pasta?

I can't.

So I tell her.

"This isn't going to work," I say.

Sara looks down at her feet, says, "You have to leave. I don't want you to see this."

"Wait, it's not like I don't understand your fear," I tell her. "It's just that I'm starting to believe you. I'm beginning to think you're going to float away if you take those things off."

Sara doesn't look up, keeps staring at her shoes until I do too. It's only then I notice they're wet with little splashes.

"Don't do that," I say to her, but what I'm thinking is, *Go on, Sara, cry your eyes out. Because I'm starting to believe you more than I should, and it's almost like the only thing keeping me here are your stupid shoes.*

"Sara," I say, and she starts to bend down.

"Wait, I understand, I do," I say. "I saw what happened to you at that amusement park. That would scare anyone."

That's when Sara really begins to cry.

She doesn't talk about what happened though, or about us. Sara begins to tell me about the butterflies. About heavy bodies. Rose petals. About light-as-a-feather souls.

Then, like Sara's had enough with dying butterflies, rose petals, and me, she begins to fiddle with her laces and I have to bend down to retie them.

But they're wet, the laces, and I'm not sure I can do it.

We drove an hour to the amusement park, taking Sara's little brother Ivan there for his 11th birthday. He played half the afternoon on some obstacle course and Sara chased him through the thing, swinging from rope to rope on it because she's fun like that.

I watched Sara jump around the course, high above the ground on a crazy assortment of ropes and nets, getting closer to catching Ivan.

I watched her lunge.

Jump.

Soar.

And, in slow motion, I watched her fall.

Sara swung over a part little kids couldn't, grasped nothing, and fell through the air, then onto her back with a wet crack, hitting her head against a piece of unprotected cement.

The blood poured out of her like a broken egg, encircling her head, and every kid and parent looked away. They assumed Sara was dead.

I did.

I thought she had to be. She was so white. Anyone who saw Sara would've thought the same thing.

She did.

Sara thought she'd died, even after the doctors stitched her up and released her from the hospital a few days later. She'd convinced herself that the only reason she hadn't floated away from this world was because her shoes were so heavy they'd kept her on the ground.

"Your body or your soul?" I'd asked.

And Sara said, "Both."

I'd bought Sara these big maroon Dr. Martens the day before the accident. We were looking for a gift for her brother and found them instead. She'd wanted them so badly that I went back and got them just so I could surprise her the next morning before we took Ivan out.

You should have seen her. The smile. She loved them.

I think they were on her mind when she fell. At least I tried telling Sara that, but she didn't believe a word. And honestly, neither did I.

In the hospital, it was touch and go the first hour. Sara had lost so much blood they didn't even have time to take her shoes off.

And all I could think then, when she was bleeding out, was that Sara's pale skin seemed a lot paler against the maroon leather, like she was a dead wicked witch who forgot to fly away before Dorothy's house crushed her, like she'd forgotten to click her red heels together one last time.

They're heavy things and Sara refuses to take them off. Therapy. Sleep. Showers. She keeps those suckers on.

Until now.

Sara unties one shoe, then the next.

Because I can't bring myself to lace them back up. I can't.

"You don't have to do that," I say. "It won't change anything. Really, it's okay."

I tell her this not because I don't want to break up, not because she wears heavy shoes or because she can't get over her fear. I tell her this because I am afraid.

Of what happens next.

I tell her it's okay, that it could be just a temporary break or not one at all.

She doesn't move when I say it, but if she were to, if you were to watch Sara walk, you'd swear she didn't lift a foot. Not at all. More like the opposite. Like she's trying to keep her feet on the ground, as if gravity no longer existed, like she has to fight to stay here, pushing one foot down after the other just to keep herself from drifting away.

She's so pale, too, if you look at her.

And really what happened to Sara could happen to anyone.

To me.

It's a thin string tethering us together.

And I understand better than she does now, I think. Because I see her struggle.

I get it, I do. I understand it's sad to see butterflies fall to the ground or red balloons float away. All of it. The rose petals, too.

So I tell her, "Don't step out of those shoes. Not for me."

But Sara, she doesn't listen.

And then it's over. Between us.

She's gone.

Just

like

th

a

t.

BLOODHOUNDS

Simon doesn't want a Golden Retriever. Not like other boys his age. What my son wants is different. "Dad," he says, "I want to *be* a dog." He's a good kid, Simon, doesn't complain about much, not my lousy dinners or my pacing the backyard as I call everyone his mother knows, so I play along with the dog thing. It's good to know what you want, I tell him, it's what your mother used to say. He shakes his head, remembering, and I wonder how much he does. Specifics from late night arguments? Sara yelling "You need to want me, Jeremy! It's not enough to need me!"? Any of that stuff could be damning. I don't want Simon to run away too, so I drop down on all fours, bite his soccer ball until he laughs and tackles me to the ground.

He's loyal. I really shouldn't worry. Simon knows what he wants, and right now he wants to be a dog.

Me? If you were to ask Sara, she'd say I was one. But that's not true. Not entirely. I don't stray. I get lost, drunk, knock over trash cans, but I never run away. What kind of dog does that? It goes against the whole notion of Man's Best Friend. If one day you get up, pack your bowl and toys, leave without a word, what kind of message does that send? What kind of tricks are you teaching?

It makes me angry to think about, which is all I've been doing.

Thinking.

About.

Runaways.

I play in the yard, kick Simon's soccer ball at the fence, keep thinking, keep kicking late into the night because no one stops me. Sara's not there to yell "Jeremy, for God's sake, come inside and make sure Simon washes up!"

I kick and kick until Simon says, "Dad, we're German Shepherds."

And then we are.

And we're vicious.

Because Simon had a bad day at school, and me, I didn't even go to work. I called every one of Sara's contacts, sent a mass e-mail to her friends. In hindsight, I should've cleaned the house, not sent the email, not left the voicemails.

Simon and I run in a circle in the backyard, working ourselves into a frenzy, nipping each other's back feet, then we bust over the fence, and later I bite our asshole neighbor Eric in the back of the leg when he steps out of his car. He falls, screaming, and I think, *Hey, that's for looking so smug when I told you Sara left.*

Simon runs. In less than a minute, he's back in our yard behind the knocked over trash cans. I meet him there, not sure if this is what he wanted until he smiles and pees on one of the cans, lifting his leg while holding onto me for balance.

"Tomorrow," he says, eyes wide with excitement, "we're Border Collies."

And we are.

In the evening, when the kids play ball in the street, we come rushing out, barking, herding them toward our garage. Simon says, "We should give these fuckers haircuts like the stupid sheep they are," and I bark at him because I'm tired, because his mother would never let him say that. Inside the garage, the kids cry while Simon circles them in the tight quarters. We open the door. Simon barks. And while the other kids run to their mothers who are home waiting for them, I howl behind them "If you talk about our game, I'll bite you!" I look at Simon and he shakes his butt like he's wagging his tail in approval.

After marking our territory around the back fence, we drink lime slushies in the kitchen. Simon flips through a dog book Sara bought him for his last birthday. She promised if he read it and studied up on the dog he wanted, how to care for it, she'd talk to me about buying him one. Now she's not here to rub my belly, to whisper to me in bed convincing me it's a good idea for Simon to have a dog. She can't do any of that because I couldn't teach her to stay.

The next morning, I tell Simon he has to go to school and he pees on the carpet. Later, I tell Simon he'd better get dressed and he steals my shoe. When I tell Simon we're not playing anymore, that I have work, he somehow gets through the fence. "Damn it, Simon, come back!" I yell. All I can do, though, is listen to the sound of his rapid feet pattering away down the street from me. I suppose I caused this. This is my fault, too, but Simon, he's loyal, so I shouldn't be surprised when he bursts back into the yard yelping and whining that he's got her scent, that we're

Bloodhounds now, that we need to move.

I drop to all fours and follow.

He traces a winding path through the back alleys, behind the houses on our street, sniffing one trash can after another until he arrives at the one that started this. Scattered before me are the contents of my neighbor Brian's trash can spilled onto the street. Simon circles a discarded wedding picture with my face on it that sits next to an empty wine bottle and a condom. On the street, my favorite Nirvana T-shirt has banana on it. Sara took that for no reason. I lift my leg, pee for what seems an eternity, drench Sara's refuse so everyone knows it's mine. The hair on my neck stands on end. My back arches.

I am not playing anymore.

The growl emanating deep from my belly is real. It is a dominance thing, keeping Simon behind me as we make our way up Brian's back drive to the door separating us from her. We stay on all fours as we approach, slinking up the back steps. I turn to Simon, but before I say it, he does. "You're a wolf now, Dad."

And I am – an animal in anger, a pack member preparing to punish one of his own. Behind me, Simon howls, and I'm not sure if he's a Bloodhound still or if Simon's remembered where all dogs come from – the wild, because that's what we are about finding her. Wild. So we salivate and move closer, letting instinct take the lead.

THE WORST THING ABOUT HELL
IS YOU HAVE TO CLIMB DOWN TO IT

At the diner, over coffee, I say, "You won't believe this story."

And you won't.

"It's about this girl and a ladder," I tell you. "Pretty hard to believe actually."

It is.

You stare. The pumpkin pie falls from your fork. You look at me, ask, "What girl? What ladder?"

You're always politer, know what to say and when.

That's why I tell you.

That, and because imagine you're me and you know this story, the one about the girl and the ladder. What would you do? Not tell it over pie? Not go home and look at the ladder in your basement?

You'd have to.

We all have to.

You pick up your fork, scoop the fallen pie back on, eat. Mouthfuls go by. The empty plate sits in front of you.

"So are you going to tell me the story?" you ask.

"No. I mean, yes."

I watch your face, checking to see if you notice I'm acting weird.

I'm nervous. About this story. I can't help it.

I'm afraid.

At night, I twist the blankets around my legs until I can't move. The tight sheets wrap around me, and it helps. The blankets around the ankles, they keep me where I should be – temporarily in bed, away from ladders and basements – but they can't stop me from going down there.

"So yesterday," I say, "the girl in apartment 6B, the cute one, Sara, who sometimes rides the elevator with us." Your eyes lock on mine wondering if she's the girl you think she is, the one who takes her hat off in the elevator as soon as the doors close.

"Did you help her with a ladder?" you ask. "She cop a feel as a thank you?"

You laugh and wait for me to do the same.

That should be funny, me being grabbed by a beautiful girl like Sara, but that's not the face I'm making.

There is no smile.

"Go on," you say.

I look over my shoulder.

No devil in the booth behind me.

"No, it's nothing crazy like that," I tell you. "We didn't exchange numbers. We didn't even say goodbye to each other."

"Why not?" you ask.

"Because she disappeared down a ladder in the building's basement."

My water spills.

It pours down the side of the table.

Maybe it sizzles when it hits the ground.

Maybe it doesn't.

You lean in and study my face for some sign of a joke. You search for a facial twitch, something indicating I'm wrong in the head.

But I'm not twitching.

I'm telling.

A story.

"The power went out on our floor in the building the other week. Usually someone goes down to the basement, flips the circuit, turns it all back on. Me, I wait until that happens and sit in the dark. Sara, though, last week, she goes down the back steps, all six floors, to the basement. When she's down there, after she flips the switch, she trips on a tile. The tile, it juts out a bit. And after she falls, she just kind of reaches down, pulls on it to see how loose it is, and it comes right up, like a trap door — and there's a ladder underneath, leading straight down into a black nothing. At least from the looks of it it's nothing. But when Sara flips on her flashlight and starts down the rungs, one after the other, she goes maybe five feet before she's all of a sudden coming down the steps of the big slide at her old elementary school, St. Augustine's. The slide's the one in the playground all the kids in her grade would stand in line to go down, the one Sara as a kid couldn't bring herself to climb up. She'd always get stuck and cry while the other kids on the playground gathered around her. She'd grit her teeth and refuse to take another step and her classmates would just scream the meanest shit about her holding up the line. They'd laugh and yell until she came back down and she always regretted it."

"How the hell do you know that?" you ask.

"She told me. But I was there too. I went to St. Augustine's. I yelled at her with the other kids. Christ, we'd chant, 'Sara Wells, go to Hell, you'll never go down the sliding board.' We'd keep saying it over and over until she'd cry. She always cried."

"That's fucked up. You were a bad kid, Sam," you say.

"I know," I tell you.

You say, "Sorry."

But you don't mean it.

You ask, "Did she keep climbing down the ladder or did she finally go up it or something?"

"Hold on, let me finish," I tell you.

I swallow a gulp of coffee.

Awful and hot.

It burns.

You should tell me this story is bull, that I'm crazy for believing some weird girl.

I want you to.

But you wait for what's next instead, like I wait in my apartment, thinking of a ladder in a basement.

"So Sara tells me all this in the elevator," I say, "that she climbs up the ladder because she's not a scared kid anymore, and — BAM — she's back in the basement. Except. She says she can't sleep. At work, she sits in front of her computer, opening new docs and typing words on an angle forming tiny steps or she repeats the letter H down the page so it looks like the ladder."

I draw the Hs on a napkin and loosen my collar.

Maybe it's hot.

You can't be sure.

"She tells me it gets so bad she goes to the basement every night, thinks about whether or not she should climb down again, and then she does."

"Yeah? Again?" you ask.

"She searches the ground, sweeps her fingers over the floor, finds the loose tile. It comes right up. And sure enough, she tells me, the ladder, there it is, leading into darkness."

"That's pretty weird," you say. "Sure she's telling the truth?"

I ignore you.

For the story's sake.

"Sara, though," I say, "she's not afraid anymore. She's climbed the rusty rungs of the big playground ladder. So she does it. Except."

"What?"

"This time when Sara goes down the ladder, she comes down attic steps and she's thirty-two. Turns out she hides Christmas presents up there for her kids, a little boy and girl. Except the girl, she looks nothing like Sara, so she might be a step child or something. Sara's not sure and up in the attic her husband hides fucked up photos Sara should call the police about. Photos she wants to cry about. Man, the photos are so bad. Then her husband tells her, like he's not hiding shit up there, to quit going up into the attic. He tells her the kids are getting suspicious about where their gifts come from, that they won't believe in Santa anymore. Then the kids come and run by her, tug at her, asking her to pull down the ladder again so they can go up there. They want to see what she's been doing up there in the attic. They smile innocent enough — but they know. They know. Those kids know what she's up to. It makes Sara's heart hurt because they're such good smiles. When her husband sweeps the kids down the hall, chasing them, making bear sounds, Sara pulls the little rope, the one that lets down the attic steps. She wants to see how many presents she got them or maybe she's going to gather the fucked up photos hidden behind the support beam. Maybe she's not ready to be married with kids. Something. She unfolds the ladder, extends the steps to the floor, up she goes."

"How many presents did she get them?" you ask.

My mouth drops.

"Don't you get how this works?" I say. "She doesn't walk up into an attic full of old boxes. There are no fucking colorfully wrapped presents. She climbs up those steps and — BAM — she's back in the basement again. Then it's up the apartment stairwell for her — almost — except Sara's afraid to go up them, the steps, so she waits ten minutes in the dark for the elevator, rides up to our floor, tells me she's glad I'm taking the elevator and not the stairs, that maybe I could hang out with her for a while or at least let her into her apartment and turn on the lights so she can be sure it's her apartment and not some other place that makes her want to cry."

I look at you, take your hand, the one with the clacking spoon stained from coffee. I make it stop shaking.

It's not shaking like mine, though.

You're excited.

You want more story.

"What does that crazy loon tell you next?" you ask. "Did she really make you turn on her light? Christ, she's desperate. All that just to sleep with you, huh? I thought she was weird, not wearing her hat in the elevator. You know, I think she purposely lets her hair down so you can see how pretty she is."

But that's not how the story goes.

"No," I tell you, "it's not like that."

You smile because you don't believe.

"She went down the ladder again," I tell you. "After that night, she told herself to get over it, to forget about the attic and the photos, the sliding board and the jeers."

"No shit," you say. "Can't believe she went down again. Christ. What did she say happened this time? What happened? What happens?"

You need to know.

You need my story.

Like I need you to believe.

"Sara," I say to you, "pounds on my door. When I open it, she pulls on my arm, tells me I have to go downstairs, that it's awful. I need to go down to the basement, to the ladder. I grab her, tell her this needs to stop, that she's not okay. I'm scared because she's so pale, like no blood in her. I'm afraid she might die right there in my doorway. She tells me I need to carry her to the elevator, that she'll never go down stairs again, that she was wrong to not be afraid. She needs a hospital. But first, Sara says, before she checks herself away, I need to check the basement just once for her because the last time she found it again, the tile, the ladder into the blackness — except when she went down the rungs, she had to stop and hold on for dear life. Why? Because the ladder, it starts moving, takes her through the darkness at an awful speed. It drives her toward this terrible orange glow in the distance. That's when, Sara tells me, she realizes she's on a fire engine. She's speeding toward this great big fire off in the distance. She has to hold on to the ladder until her hands go white, until her fingernails bite so deeply into her palm they draw blood. And no shit, I look at her palms, and they're bloody. They're so fucking bloody. She starts to cry in my doorway, muttering about how the fire engine slams through a wall of flame, how fire spreads everywhere, all around her, that the ladder she's on, the one extended high into the darkness above those flames, it drops and — BAM — she's in the basement again. But she's not so sure anymore. And her hands are bleeding. And she thinks she might be on fire or dead or something."

You don't speak.

I don't either.

My hands hurt.

The burns blister.

The waitress wants to know if we plan on paying.

You keep your eyes on mine, say to her, "Sure, we'll leave a big tip."

"What did you do?" you ask. "Did you go down there like she asked?"

You liked the story earlier.

Now you're not sure.

"I took her to the hospital first," I say. "I carried her to the elevator and she cried the entire ride down, shaking and holding me."

What I don't tell you is: Sara's hair, her curls, loose around my face, smelled like smoke.

She reeked.

And so do I.

You stare at me, notice I'm not telling you something.

My clothes are dirty with soot.

"Your shirt," you say, "it's burnt."

"Couldn't find another," I tell you. "The power, it went out this morning."

You nod.

You're figuring out the rest.

How it ends.

"My apartment was totally black," I tell you. "Had to take the stairs down to the basement, to flip the circuit."

You're looking into my eyes, watching the tears, seeing the end, how the story finishes. It's me tripping in the darkness down in the basement.

It's me finding a loose tile.

It's me climbing down to so many different hells.

Some I've known.

Some in a future not worth living.

So many hells so much worse than I thought — and you, you see them now.

You know how the story ends.

It's with you.

Because now you know.

Now you'll climb

down

    H

    H

    H

    H

    Hell, you know you have to. You know I'll show you the way.

And I do.

Down the ladder you go.

And you're six and your dad stays asleep on the sofa even though the EMT tries his hardest.

Down you go and you're in your college dorm and you pretend you can't hear her because the music is too loud.

Down

and

down

you

go

until you see the fire too.

Because it's your story now.

Not mine.

THE GREATER MIGRATION

When the shuttle blasted, launching me outside Earth's orbit, it wasn't Sara I thought of, or even the kids – it was the PBS animal documentary on migrating albatrosses.

I'd been sitting in my family room the evening prior with the lights dimmed, a pillow propped against my chest for security. Both Jason and Gayle had fallen asleep next to me. Sara leaned over, wrapped her arm about my neck, kissed me, saying "Don't worry about it, spaceman. I'll put them to bed. What's one more night?"

I got the message, carried Jason to bed, kissed his forehead, thought how I might die in space, that this might be the last time I saw him.

I kissed Jason again, fluttered over to Gayle's doorway, held Sara there, as light as air. We watched our little darling Gayle breathe in, breathe out, our own repetition matching her falling chest.

Later I sat back on the sofa, watched television, absorbed the details. The albatross flew across the Atlantic. It used thermo updrafts from islands along the way to gain great height; the warm land baking under the sun produced an advantage to soar from, drifting the bird across, away to where it wanted – needed – to go.

In the shuttle, I considered the moon. How I would soon walk on it, ending the first half, the greatest half, of the journey.

The dangerous trip was always half-drifting home.

On the moon, walking the surface, I thought of the albatross, not Sara, as I watched the speck come closer.

Sara would've grabbed the back of my arm, squeezed, pulled me near, whispered "I love you. I love you and Jason and little Gayle. No matter what. Okay?"

Sara would have pulled me away from the speck, telling me to snap out of it, to stop staring and start walking, to forget about how far things will travel to get to where they need to go.

Except the speck now seemed to contain two tiny shooting stars within it, and it was hard to look away.

I stood, the breathing reverberating in my suit, soft echoes calling me to live and come home.

I stared, mission control temporarily silenced, awaiting my word.

I told them "Control, there is definitely something coming toward me."

"Roger. We need the size of the meteorite relative to your hand and the distance between it and your helmet. Count the seconds before the meteor appears larger than your fist. If it doesn't appear significantly larger in five, then it's not going to hurt you."

"It's a bird."

"What?"

When I'd forgotten about Sara, about Jason and little Gayle, when the speck coasting through space stayed as large as my left hand, I watched it, a silver bird, drift into the moon's orbit, break through the almost nonexistent gravitational pull there. I watched it land, like I had, on the moon's surface, only feet from where I stood. It fluttered its wings once. Not like a bird from Earth – it rippled. The bird, I told Control, turned its head, a silky glob of soft metal, and stared at me with stars for eyes. A small, sharp point like the tip of kitchen knife squawked at me without sound. Its feathers rippled, perpetually in motion, pouring themselves into the mold of something similar to a sparrow made of mercury. And then, with another ripple, its own unique form of fluttering, the little silver bird lifted itself an inch off the surface of the moon.

When it landed again, its sharp point beak pecked at the moon rocks, then its own chest. It stretched liquid wings, waves in weightlessness, before it decided to move on. I explained to Control how the bird had begun to ripple larger than before, that this great ripple coursed through its small bird's body, that thousands of miniature aftershocks followed. I noted to Control that the bird's body was an ocean, wave after wave, some sort of little silver tsunami, and that the motion of which somehow launched it into flight, upward to the reaches of space where it continued to ripple before me, maintaining its flight momentarily before becoming motionless, a tear of silver soaring in orbit, floating from one moon to the next.

By the time I stopped thinking of PBS, of the albatross flying over great expanses of ocean, drifting from one island to the next, the silver speck with stars for eyes had flown farther away from the Moon, and Mission Control wanted me to dump oxygen from my suit, to board the shuttle, saying "It's time to come back home. You need a little solid ground beneath your wings."

THIS KID'S LIGHTNING

When I was little, I couldn't see. Not a thing. Not my dead sister Sara, my mom, or the sky. In front of me there was a greatness so black and vast that you would've thought it was death. That's where I played with the rabbits and made myself seen.

In the dark, a blind boy can find all sorts of things other people can't. When my mother called "Where's the remote?" to me in the night, I found it. It was sitting next to her on the floor by our Labrador, Oodles. Hey, boy, get out of the way. Mom needs this.

I needed nothing. Not even a flashlight. Except when it rained.

Thunderstorms sounded an alarm for me. Inside my chest a pounding clock would bump, counting down until the lightning struck. When it did, I could see everything.

But just during those flashes.

I could see my best friends the rabbits, hurrying to get to their holes. Once I even saw my mom talking to my dead sister, just sitting there on Sara's unmade bed, next to the window, beside herself with guilt.

Before I was blind, I had a pet rabbit, black as the night. He was outside and I was in. And when it started to storm, I'd get scared for him, all alone inside his cage with only a roof to shelter him away from the wind.

I'd run to him and make sure he was alright.

One time when I ran to him, into the night of wind, rain, and lightning, I was dressed like a knight wearing tin foil and pans. I had a television antennae I'd found in the garage, extended to its full height. And with my lance held high, I stormed out and was promptly struck down by God.

He blinded me and freed my rabbit. It was a sin. I blew right into the hutch, broke my arm and dislocated my shoulder.

My mother cried in the hospital and apologized about not being there to stop me.

She said she was sorry I couldn't see anymore and that we could go home the next day.

She was wrong.

I dressed like a knight because it felt good to swing my sword and free the villagers. The night I went blind I wanted to save her, my mom, from her boyfriend, to stop her from going to his lair.

It was hours before the strike.

I charged out of the house to see her car pulling down the driveway, dust and gravel kicked up by how fast she drove to him.

I waved my antennae in the air and shouted "Who goes there?!" but if she saw me in the rearview mirror, she didn't stop. She kept on toward him, so I kept standing in the road, in the gravel and the dust.

After the wake of her car subsided, I entered my house through the front door and sat down on the sofa.

I can still do that. Without looking.

The rain the night I went blind pounded into the ground so hard that I kept thinking it was my mother running up the porch steps and pounding on our front door.

When the wind whirled around the house in such a way that I thought I was Dorothy and that was the day I would fly away, I ran out the front with a hard right toward the hutch.

When the lightning shattered me and threw me and took away what I thought was mine, I was holding my antennae lance, feet away from what once was my black-as-night pet rabbit.

When the lightning took away my sight and my breath and almost my life, I did nothing more than seize in a puddle and have a nosebleed. I didn't even swing my sword.

I could tell my ears were bleeding too because they were warmer than the rain and nothing sounded the same. Not even the ground.

After a shudder and a pulse, I listened to the beating rain and considered my blindness.

And the lightning flashed. I saw beads of water, thousands coming down on me.

Then, a blackness so vast.

And the lightning flashed. There was the broken hutch, twisted wire and splinters.

Then a dark so deep you would've thought it was death.

And the lightning flashed. It showed me everything I needed to see.

It crackled and sounded like bees in my head, a blue-white streak zigzagging from Heaven, hitting the field far away, letting me watch my little black rabbit disappear through the grass. He made it to a hole in the ground no more than six feet away under a tree. Vanished. Free.

The holes rabbits run to, shelter away in and live out their lives in, are networking tunnels that go on and about, so far and so winding that only the family members who belong there know where the holes start and where they end.

After the hospital, I would lie there in the same spot where I crashed into the hutch and fell to the ground, my ear to the scorched earth. I didn't hear a thing there so I had to move closer to where they were beneath the tree.

I asked my mother to help me find the hole. It wasn't hard for her.

Then, I heard the warren. I heard all the rabbits.

I was worried they would reject mine, fail to make him their king. But one afternoon he emerged. My mother saw him. She told me.

She shouted and described what I should've seen.

She wanted me to see him. She told me where he was in the yard, that there were other rabbits following him. Then he was gone, she said, down the hole.

I pressed my ear to the ground right there, near their home, to listen to his sounds. There was a whole family of rabbits living and loving and taking care of each other. I could hear them, even the black one who they loved most of all.

WHAT I LEARNED
BENEATH YOUR SHIRT

After the accident, I could no longer pronounce the word *trouble*. My *t*s did not exist. No longer did the sound of hot tamales fall off the tongue – all I could say was *rubble*. It was as close to the word *trouble* as I could muster and it seemed to fit my place.

The *t* sound that I'd been so accustomed to came out my pursed lips like a little pocket of air, nothing there but breath. But at least, she told me, I was living. "A breath in place of a *t*," she said, "is a good thing, you know."

"Like when poe-s coun syllables?" I asked her, ashamed I could no longer make others understand how beautiful I could be.

After the accident, she was a visiting nurse from the cancer ward who spent the night with me, making my hands trace along the paper what my lips couldn't quite understand as if, when I'd regained the use of my fingers and could write again, my mind would somehow recognize all that it could do with the tongue.

I told her, "You don' undersand. You jus can' fathom wha I'm feeling righ now," and she took my hand and put it beneath her blouse and I felt something else instead. It was warm. It was sensual. It was beautiful. And there was only one. The absence of the other was recognizable from the space between my finger and my thumb.

I knew then what she had already known and had not bothered to say.

I said, "You're rubble,"

and she told me, "You don' undersand. You jus can' fathom wha I'm feeling righ now."

We laughed, then smiled, then kissed. We knew we understood what the other was trying to say. She was trouble – the only kind I could pronounce.

We wrote a poem together in the hospital, called it "Living."

If you had a dagger for every time you stabbed at a thief,
you'd be a dangerous man.
A wronged woman.
And I wouldn't stab at you or steal from you at all.

If you had a sword for every time you stabbed at a king,
you'd have a shield
– no sword at all –
because their knights are scary upon their horses,
high above the ground, charging toward you.
Kings make the laws.
And they're all men who have no trouble pronouncing their words
or their sentences.

If you had a word for every time I had a story,

we would call each other more,
converse and lie,
tell each other what was wrong and what was fine.
It's been a day.
It's been a week.
It's been way too long.

If I had a month to tell you everything I should have told you,
I'd be on a horse riding into town,
telling you the cancer treatment is free.

If I knew life and you knew God,
we'd call them both thieves and say, "I have a dagger for you.
Don't you dare look the other way."

She wanted to read it at a coffee shop around the corner. When we arrived, I tried to leave. She took me by the hand and brought me to the front of the room. I stared at her blouse, at the rhythm of her breast, breathing steadily for the both of us.

I changed the name of the poem without telling her. She smiled when she heard me say it – *rubble* – right into the microphone.

She was the only one in the room who understood like I did, and later that night when we shared ourselves with each other, I left my hand on what remained of her chest, knowing the title change didn't really matter.

I THINK I'M GOING TO MAKE IT

Other people have nightmares. I have the sleepy hahas. I wake up laughing.

And I'm happy for it.

When my eyes open, I'm beneath the covers, sweating, panting, holding my sides. I can't stop. Don't want to. It helps me remember my father and everything else that's not funny.

I can laugh at my dreams, laugh at my pain, laugh at the others, the hell they have to go through, as if it's funny.

And it is.

When Simon, dying of cancer, sits in bed in a hospital, his painful condition making me want to get up in the middle of the night to drive over to his wife and kids, I laugh instead.

When he asks "What will my family do? How much will my son cry? When my heart stops, will I feel a pain as great as the love I have for my boy?" it's too funny, so I laugh like a man bleeding out onto his own hospital sheets, like there's life and death everywhere, all over me, and I can't stand how funny it is to look at.

It's the ridiculousness of death that helps the chortles turn to deep-bellied hysterics, and I laugh like I'm a ten-year-old boy.

I'm laughing, Dad. Still.

Thanks to you.

I'm laughing like I've got nothing to lose, and, in a way, I don't. I lost it when you fell. Of course, I was a boy, and had – and still do have – lots in front of me in terms of life, but what I mean is that I lost *it*.

It was the will to take life as something controllable, something serious despite my inability to know where I was going, what would happen next.

It was my little feet pounding down a hiker's path somewhere in Pennsylvania.

It was following my mother away from where you'd fallen.

It was nothing more than that, so I laugh at it whenever I can, like it's the funniest part of life there is – death, dying, and the distance in between.

That sense of good, respectable fear, it fell down a ravine and yelled "I think I'm going to make it" at the top of its lungs, laughing all the way down.

And thank goodness.

Thanks, Dad.

It was an accident, tragic, an awful sight for any child, but you thought to make it funny – and I'm still smiling.

I cried for days, waking up each night laughing my head off. Mom would run to my room, hold me, cry.

It hurt because I laughed. It upset her because you fell into a ravine.

She never saw me cry, though. I never let her, never

wanted her to see my face full of hurt. You tried your best, Dad, to stop me from feeling that, so why let her see? Why let you down? You'd already traveled so far, so fast, there wasn't much farther you could go.

I couldn't do that to you, so I did my best to hide away what wasn't funny.

It was easy at night, when the dream would come. I'd walk behind you. You'd laugh, say, *Come on guys, catch up! This is going to be great!* Then you'd run ahead, push through dead bramble. And on the other side, the edge of the ravine, every time, I'd watch you walk right off, see the terror on your face, the sudden realization there was nothing underneath you. I'd watch a face of fear change into something absurd, something funny, like what was happening was the funniest thing you'd ever thought of.

You did that for me.

When you stepped out to where you were sure a path existed, you lead us to the edge of a ravine instead, and fell – but you made it right.

You made it a joke to stop us from crying.

But also because it was funny.

Because it was hilarious. And you knew it and so do I.

I think I'm going to make it. I yelled it too, but in my sleep, down the hall from Mom, alone in her room.

And it was terrible, funny, sad.

It was you, Dad.

Every time.

When they found your body, I bet it looked hilarious. I mean, you fell into a ravine and giggled – why wouldn't you be a mess of a man, smiles and broken teeth, waiting for your boy at the bottom?

You must have understood life better than most, or at least you must have understood grief because when you fell, you ruined the whole concept of sadness and death.

You ruined tragedy.

There are theaters with dramatic masks out front where one cries and the other laughs. Those places are wrong. They don't understand there's only one face and it can be found at the bottom of a ravine in Pennsylvania.

The night my mother came to my room and I cried as she held me against her shoulder, she laughed.

She told me, "I think I'm going to make it." She said it through tears and chokes, and I cried so hard we were both wet and she laughed so hard we held each other, repeating your joke, a holy chant separating us from what had happened, keeping us safe at the top, far from the bottom.

CAVEMEN UNTIL BLUE

Outside, in the rain, behind the house, huddled, crouched down near the shed, you don't see me. I'm there, though, doing a line of semi-wet coke and asking Jimmy whether the acid should have kicked in yet. He reminds me it's not acid, that it's a new chemical compound we're trying and that we're supposed to blog about it tomorrow or else it won't be free.

"Scientists," he says. "We're like scientists doing research."

But we're nothing like that.

We're using street drugs – variations – to experience something greater than our own realities. Until tonight. Tonight I find the blue and become part of you.

But before *you*, before *us*, when it's me traversing the universe alone behind your grandfather's house, Jimmy encourages me to think as if I'm a researcher bettering mankind, not an addict breaking in for a score, so I say "I'm not a fucking scientist. I'm a Neanderthal at best, clubbing my crude way along for survival," and Jimmy shakes his head because I don't get the big picture, only cute, lifelike drawings of tigers attacking cavemen on subway station walls. That's just how I am before the blue.

"Fuck, you don't know a thing," Jimmy says and lights up a glass pipe full of something no scientist would approve of.

He's right, too. I have no idea why I'm covered in rain, watching your window. "Come on," he says, "we're going in through the back door."

And we do.

Inside, our flashlights shine thin beams of light onto kitchen appliances and Jimmy says, "The guy brings the shit home from his lab and stores it here in his own fucking office."

"What is it?" I ask, but I don't care because I don't listen when Jimmy explains that the guy makes something new – something special, something different. Instead, I raise my hammer, the one I hold in my left hand, because there is a man in a lab coat standing in front of me whose eyes glow neon blue and when he speaks little wisps of electric blue smoke escape his lips.

"There you are," he says, but I'm already closing the distance and bringing down the hammer in all its crudeness.

On the floor, the scientist Jimmy somehow knows lies still and I can see a hint of the blue glow behind his closed eyes.

"Is he dead?" Jimmy asks, making his way over the body to the stairs.

"No, I don't think so. I don't know," I say.

Upstairs, you sit alone in your grandfather's office. You huddle in the corner, understanding that something has happened below in the kitchen.

You can feel it.

The blue pulses through you and your grandfather, connecting you to him, him to you, making it as if you were momentarily struck with a hammer and, as if your grandfather weren't lying on the kitchen floor downstairs but in fact huddled upstairs, being as much you as you are him, part of the growing blue.

And when I find you, Jimmy stands there next to you saying he doesn't understand. He points at your little blue glowing body. "What the fuck is this?" he asks. I shrug, stare into your blue, fixate on the intensity of your eyes. You search through me with a hot blue-white fever, and I see the universe. In the dark of the room, the incandescent pale of your blue body creates the same effect glacier ice has in dark water – it illuminates and attracts, calling my vessel to it, so I step a foot forward using your eyes as stars to navigate by.

We're connected.

In the dark, your eyes crackle like live wire sparks, zapping against a wet street.

In my head, I hear you, your grandfather too – "This is evolution" – and those words, *our* words, it's an electric unison, a soft fuzz humming around syllables, empowering them, and it makes perfect sense to me, words I can feel vibrating in my head.

Perfect sense.

"What the fuck are you doing?" Jimmy yells, but I don't care. I don't listen. You outstretch your hand, offer me a little blue cube, radiant, pulsating, formed from your palm. "Is that it?" Jimmy yells. "Is that the goddamn compound?" He grabs you by your little blue shoulders and I bring down the hammer against his head. In my other hand, I hold the cube, and when I open it, it absorbs into our skin leaving a blue square to mark our palm.

By the time our eyes start to flicker, our grandfather walks into the room illuminated and we feel less like us and more like the rain outside. And by the time we begin to glow, like you, skin and all, we wonder together in our blue mind if we should show our friends this, if they will understand we're an ocean, that they should learn to swim in us, to dip into our radiant blue existence and become something blue, something more than their caveman struggle to survive out there alone.

We wonder, we blue, we wonder.

YOUR UNCLE SCOTT
IS A LAKE MONSTER

"Why do you think Uncle Scott's the monster?" Simon asks as we pull the car off the road and onto the dirt path between the dying pine trees.

I don't answer.

Simon doesn't question me again until I turn the low beams off and tell him to grab our headlamps from the back seat.

"Are you sure?" he asks.

"It's your Uncle Scott," I tell him. "He's the monster drowning them."

No reply.

He doesn't want to understand.

That's okay.

"Simon," I say, "we're bounty hunters tonight, catching the crazy."

He nods in the dark.

No laughter.

I shouldn't have said that.

Simon squirms in his seat.

I don't. No moving. Only imagining.

But my shoes are wet. I'm sure of that. The squeak from the rubber hurts. It resonates and pounds in my head as I ease my foot off the brake.

So I put my hand on Simon's shoulder and he smiles.

It makes me feel better.

That smile means not needing to say "Simon, one day you might be a monster, too. It runs in the family." But when I turn my headlamp on, the light shines on Simon and I realize he isn't smiling.

I imagined what I wanted to see again.

That's how it is – me imagining, seeing things, and this is happening, and oh well, and oh God, so I let the light pour from my headlamp until it spots an old Ford pickup tucked between two pines off the dirt road.

It's Scott's truck.

"Dad, that's not Uncle Scott's. That's Mom's van."

"Don't reply."

"What?"

No reply.

"Dad?"

I don't reply.

Simon doesn't understand.

I can hear the lake. The waves. They're close.

Simon cries next to me. He uses his arm to wipe away the tears.

The sleeve looks heavy, like army surplus, like wool logged with water.

It's not wet. I know that. But it's hard to be sure.

Simon continues to wipe away tears. There are so many.

From the backseat, I pull the hammer. I'm prepared to use it. I considered a hatchet, but it's my brother.

The rope and duct tape I throw in the backpack.

The crossbow I give to Simon.

He takes it in his hands, points it at me, keeps it aimed at my face.

We stare at each other until I stop thinking about his mother and the lake and say, "Damn it, Simon, not at me."

Simon points the bow down, sighs.

He sounds exhausted, like a swimmer dying or like a hundred-pound person pushed under a thousand-pound water balloon. A smothered nothing. An exhale.

His headlamp turns away, glaring out the window onto the crumbling wood of the rotted sign reading Darlyn Lake.

I wonder if he remembers summers here where we swam with Uncle Scott and his cousins, warm days where we splashed at the edge with his mother.

I wonder if he remembers Jillian like I remember her, or does he remember her like I remember my mother.

I try not to think of them.

Simon doesn't ask about his grandmother, why she's never in the photos.

I appreciate that.

The most we've discussed was my saying "You would've liked her. She was sweet," and his asking if she died early.

How do I tell my son his grandmother disappeared swimming in the lake?

I don't.

The water looks choppy. I can see it through the trees.

My brother Scott and I knew something else about Lake Darlyn and our father – not exactly, not at first. We knew something about Dad and the lake others couldn't.

Other people, they didn't know our father kept getting lost on his way to work that year, that he was angry at the trees in the yard.

Sometimes he'd stare at the sun for an hour.

He'd tell us he talked to Sergeant, that we'd better get back to work and dig the latrine.

He grabbed me by the shoulders once, pushed me to the ground. "Get the fuck down, idiot! Do you want them to see us?" He held me there, his heavy arm across my back and we lay in the grass for almost an hour while he scanned the yard for something only he could see.

I remember how impossible it was for me to move under his weight, how thankful I was when we quit the struggle and I could still breathe.

It was only grass he held me in.

No water filled the lungs.

It didn't matter much. Those things happened. Dad held us down, hid us from unseen dangers. He'd snap out of it, embarrassed, confused, not knowing how the hell we ended up on the ground in the backyard. It was hard for him to understand why his arms held us so hard beneath him, but it didn't matter – not until he came home crying, saying he couldn't find her in all the water, in that terrible fucking lake.

I remember him shouting over and over about the lake like it was real, a person who'd taken Mom from him.

I shared a look with Scott.

Our eyes said Dad did it.

He probably had an episode out in the lake surrounded by the dying pines. They stood like summer dried soldiers on a front line.

Of course Dad did it.

He'd found himself alone in the water, unable to make sense of it.

That night I cried in my pillow.

Scott said, "He's so crazy, Dad probably thinks she swam away or the lake ate her."

I laughed between sobs and thought about how deep the water was.

Six months after Mom disappeared, I sat on the concrete floor, alone in the garage, working on my bicycle with a creaking wrench in my hand.

And I felt him behind me.

My father stood there, as if from nowhere, looking at me below him. His hammer in his left hand. He stared at me. A little through me. At something I couldn't see then.

He'd look from it, then back to me, staring at what only he could see, as if I were connected to some perceived danger.

He cracked his neck, wiped his nose.

Then he said it. His thin wet whisper. "You're one of them, you devil gunner."

His pupils had taken over the eyes, so I didn't try to see if my father was somewhere inside the twitching thing standing over me.

I closed my eyes and felt the weight of the wrench in my hand, hoping it wouldn't hurt him.

Whatever happened after that happened. The memory is blackness. It is hot noise, anger, and other things I choose not to remember.

Scott said I shouldn't remember. I wouldn't forgive myself. He said "I'm your brother no matter what" and

"Let's not look at each other different, okay? It had to happen."

It didn't matter. When Dad went missing, no one checked the lake.

Scott told them Dad yelled something about going to find Mom and slammed the front door. We knew the police – everyone, actually – felt sorry for him. They thought he'd lost it over our mother's disappearance, because they knew, like we did, she was probably dead at the bottom of Lake Darlyn.

In the woods, walking to Scott's cabin, the lake shimmers. The dying pines still line the shore. I imagine they are my father in his uniform, the one he wore in summer when he had no reason to. It was hot. He was wilted. The heavy wool jacket. The green of the coat made it seem natural to be so heavy-armed and crazy.

Darlyn is cold water. It's moonlight and rolling mercury. It's a child's broken thermometer emptied into the palm, a draught of madness I should avoid.

"I don't think your mother ran away," I say to Simon. "Something worse. The lake, the fucking lake," I tell him.

My headlamp catches confusion, anger, disgust.

I remember the danger.

Scott stands in the trees. I can see him.

"No, he's not. He's not there," Simon tells me.

He shakes my arm.

"He's out there," I say. "The monster. That fucking lake. He's out there."

When I grab the back of Simon's neck so he'll understand, when I tell Simon "Stop pointing the crossbow at me," I hear a branch break and let go.

Simon runs.

I can see Scott in my father's uniform, standing along the shore of Darlyn.

He's between the trees.

I can hear my mother in the water.

Jillian, my wife, is screaming, trying to keep above the waves.

"We need to find Uncle Scott, save your mother!" I yell at the woods.

Simon keeps running.

The trees nod.

The lake swallows.

The weather is hot and my shirt scratches the arms.

I hate wool.

The color green like the army, the army like my father, my father like the grass he held me down in until I cried and he woke up.

I hate myself.

The light from Simon's headlamp bounds off the path ahead of me, shining through the trees until, for whatever reason, he turns it off, and then it's dark, and then I do what I have to and make my way to Scott's cabin, and I see him there. In uniform.

Limbs in those sleeves are fifty-pound weights.

His face is wet.

Through the window, inside my brother's house, Simon waves his arms frantically, yelling things at Scott I can't hear.

Thin strands of hair stick to his old forehead. They can't hide the sunburn from his standing in the yard.

Scott is in my father's uniform.

His arms look heavy.

I can feel the weight of the wrench in my hand.

When I look down, it's a hammer.

I am not holding a wrench.

I am not a boy in the garage.

My arms itch from wool.

"Shoot him, Simon!"

With my hammer, I smash the window.

When they turn and look through the broken glass, my father's face doesn't seem right. It looks like my brother's.

Jillian screams from the water.

The lake rumbles.

Simon scratches his face, his arm stretches in the heavy green wool of my father's uniform.

My wife is not here.

Scott is screaming, shaking Simon, telling him to do it, that I'm gone.

Simon?

I can see my father aiming the crossbow at me.

"I'm not a devil gunner!"

No reply.

My wife is not here.

I am not a devil gunner.

I don't want to be here. I hate the lake. I hate the garage.

Simon and the crossbow, and my father and the lake, and me, and–

A twang and a thud. The crossbow unburdened.

Scott looks relieved. Simon looks sad. My father looks like me when I'm close to the lake, my reflection in the ripples.

I hate the water.

Simon's arrow aches in my side and Lake Darlyn accepts me, reaches out and wraps me in its waves.

Scott can tell Simon about my father.

He can explain the lake.

The weight of Darlyn is on my shoulders, touching my neck.

I'll go and get Mom.

Dad can swim in Darlyn until then.

Simon, too.

I'll be waiting, doing the backstroke and humming stars while the pines stand guard for monsters.

While the pines stand guard.

For monsters.

AFTER-SCHOOL SPECIAL

It's weird. The girl on TV described it as feeling like a pistol being shot next to your ear. She said she couldn't hear a thing as she ran through, and that the entire place went silent a long time after. The girl on TV said she was dirt spit out of a hot airless vacuum and that when she emerged you wouldn't recognize her. She told the viewers that everyone's mouths looked like evil puppetry and that her grandma was probably screaming "No!" but she couldn't be sure. She could only deduce what had been said from the fact that the eighty-year-old woman had tried to stop her from going back in a second time.

No one tried to stop me and I could hear everything. People weren't screaming. No one said a word. If they had, it would have been too late. Whatever they said to me would have been lost inside that vacant and burning house.

And what was there to say? There were no cameras. Not even a cat.

The girl on TV said that it was the most liberating and

exhilarating sensation to ever wash over her body. She described it as if it were the ocean's last wave before the tide changes. She said that it was something on the verge of something else and that it was the most wonderful she had ever felt.

I wanted wonderful.

I wanted something else.

And after four years of nothing, I wanted to be asked what it felt like to be alive.

The girl on TV said she'd do it again, too, if given the chance.

That's probably why she's still allowed to talk about it all these years later. It's probably why she's on TV and I'm not.

Me, I would never do it again, not like that. I'd been so ignorant, taking for granted that I'd make it through the dark and out into the backyard where the sun would be shining on and on.

I'm terrified now just to pass through doorways. My dreams are filled with black smoke and I constantly take wrong turns in houses that I've never been in. I'm always ending up in the bathroom or the kid's room or the kitchen. In my dreams, I never find the back door. Those kinds of turns haunt me whenever they can. Those are the dreams waiting for me when I come home from school now. I'm afraid to take naps in the afternoon. I'm afraid for grandparents and their cats.

Her story was a little different. Hers was a freak electrical fire on the other side of town. Hers was to save the day and her grandma's Russian Blue named Dostoy. The girl on TV was crazy for going back inside, but she ended up better for it. The girl on TV realized her mistake somewhere between the family room and the kitchen. Not every kid walks home past her grandma's house. Not every kid ends up on TV for charging through a single home engulfed in flames only to emerge out the other side.

Some kids realize their mistakes halfway.

I heard everything when I ran through the house. I was on the other side of town, though, far from where the girl on TV lived with her Grandma. Maybe that's the difference between the burnings, the other side. After starting the fire, I walked back up the street a bit so it had time to breathe. It wasn't her grandmother's house or mine. I hope it wasn't any family's at all. But from what I understand from the officials, the house belonged to no one. That's probably why I chose it. That's probably why I didn't end up like the girl on TV. I dropped my book bag onto the cement. I walked up calm and collected to the burning front door. Before running through, I took a deep breath and listened for the ocean and waited for the tide to change.

A burning home to confused bystanders who don't see or hear a cat inside sounds like a crazy whoosh of hot air and sirens. To me, it sounded more like television static than like a pistol exploding beside your ear, somewhere close to your temple, far from the other side of the house or from the girl on TV. Just a loud static going on and on and on.

IN YOUR FATHER'S BACKYARD

The girl Sara who sings while at work needs to stop it with the song "I'll Be There" because it's killing me. I'll die if she doesn't learn a new tune.

She sings like something's there, something special, like she knows a place where people wait around all day just for you, and the song, her voice, it reminds me I haven't found anything like that, that maybe I should.

The girl who sings while at work is not a bad person or my first choice, but at dinner we talk about her father. She orders clams and I drink most of the wine without offering any.

"Do you have another bottle, maybe of white?" she asks. I pretend not to hear because I don't want the subject to change. I want to know him, her father.

She mentions he had everything he ever wanted, that he hid it away.

"I'll Be There" says her father is a horrible man, that I'd hate him. She stares at my empty glass, says her father drank an awful lot too, that I could thank the good lord I'd never meet him.

He lives far from here, she says, near Mexico.

I remind her we're not far from Mexico ourselves. She giggles, says, "Yeah, but when I think of my father, I think of desperadoes and buried treasure. I think of loot hidden in the hills behind my father's house."

"Your backyard sounds like a treasure trove," I say.

"According to my father," she says, "it's there."

"Don't you believe him?"

"Oh, I have no doubt he did it. I just think he's the meanest man alive. Who has everything they ever wanted and buries it somewhere for someone else to find?"

"What was it?" I ask.

She drops a clam shell down on her plate and the clink sounds like a gold coin or maybe something breaking.

Inside my pickup truck I open the other bottle of wine, stare at the napkin in my hand. Scribbled on it are the words *Treasure Father, 97 South Water Lane, Ten Springs, New Mexico.*

Her father's address is an X on my map, which I've made with a thick black pen, repeating the process – X X X – until there's no mistaking the importance of my destination.

Around the X are details put there by the map-maker: foothills, valleys, ravines, mountains, a river. Her father's backyard has it all.

And really, it isn't that far – maybe a night's drive, eight hours tops. I'll need that time to imagine exactly what I'll be finding, what I'll be doing with it when I finally have it.

"I'll Be There" says her father was super smart with a hell of a lot of sad mixed in, that he was loving and crazy, with a broken heart he didn't bother to repair.

"Empty heart," I say, because I understand before she says her mother died that it wasn't broken.

"There's a difference," I tell her.

"I'll Be There" says, "He just cried all the time. I mean, go out. Christ, find someone new, if not for you, for your family's sake, right?"

When she uses that singsong voice of hers like it's the soulful chorus of the man's life, a thing her father failed at, I know why he liquidated her mother's fortune, buried whatever it was somewhere way the hell out in his back-yard.

Whatever it was.

"I'll Be There" says he's hidden it in the desert some-where behind their house, maybe up the mountain between her back door and her father's favorite hunting spot on the ridge.

"It's probably across the river in Mexico," she says. "My parents loved it there."

"Probably," I say. "What did he hunt?"

She shrugs, says, "He never bagged anything, not for all the trouble it took him. Spent all that time alone with nothing to show for it."

"Nothing?" I ask.

"He didn't really start until after my mom died. Pro-bably wasn't even hunting. Probably had himself a whore."

She smiles like it's a wonderful joke, her father and his alone time, his possible woman.

Then "I'll Be There" says, "He'd walk straight out the back door, up the mountain, and be gone before I'd even get to say bye."

She says it like it's a bad thing, like her father wasted the better part of his life doing something even stupider than playing daddy to a terrible one-song daughter, so I shake my head because I don't want her to know I think the world of her father. I don't want her to guess he's going to give me something worth being there for.

I want it all to myself.

Inside her father's hunting lodge, I find nothing – empty bottles, pictures. It's sad, but the couch is by far the saddest. You see where he wore it away, sleeping, turning, reliving old dreams, ones he probably shared with his wife. It's bleak, the lodge, enough so that I want to leave, go back to work, apologize for not showing up the last two days – but the pictures of her father, they're great.

Because he's not alone. Not in any of them.

Her mother's there, in every one. A lot of the photos show them crossing a river in a canoe. They're kissing, holding each other, smiling by a tree. Always across the river, in Mexico, boat tied to the same tree, every picture. It's gnarled, close to the river bank, looks like a Mexican Pine.

And I think it's Christmas – finally, at last – because I know where he hid it.

I use her father's map to find the boat, repeat the process of marking my destination with the X, unpin it from his lodge wall, fold it, put it in my pocket. Done.

Later, when I pull it out again just to make sure the X is still there, I think of her mother laughing, drawing a little boat on the map to mark what she loved so they'd never forget where it was, then I picture her father covering her little drawing of a boat with a picture of her still smiling in a little pink tee, so he'd never forget her.

It makes me sad to think of him in his cabin, crying, dreaming about what he had. I hope I find it, something better even. I hope it's not what I think it's gonna be.

I think of him, his wife, about them smiling in the photos, their daughter singing "I'll Be There," and wonder where I am and really just where it is I think I'm going.

Later, when I untie their red canoe, my hope is that it works long enough to float me across, that I don't drown in something so old. I can find my own way back once I have it, if what I want is there, if it's not what I think it's gonna be.

Beneath the Mexican Pine there's a piece of frayed rope. It's tied around the trunk, not enough to secure to. I drag the canoe up, sit it down by the tree. I wonder if storms, flood waters, if time itself raised the river high enough to wash away the bank at the roots, if maybe I won't have to search for what her father hid so long ago.

It might not even be here if that's the case. It could have washed away downriver. Then at least I can delude myself, keep thinking whatever it is I haven't found is still worth looking for.

Carved into the tree, the classic heart, one name worn away, the other etched deep – *Sara*. Both there in their own way.

It's here.

I know for sure now.

I find it after two hours of digging. Two hours of anything is enough and I'm glad her father must have felt the same way.

I open the bottle of wine, drink.

In my hands, pictures of happier days, love letters signed XOXO, a pile of dirt. Most of what's here is ruined. It's what I thought it would be – it's everything her father had, probably the most expensive bottle of wine I've seen.

Everything you have and love, you bury. Everything you stumble across or dig up in life is amazing until it's gone.

There are a couple of signed checks at the bottom. Worthless. They have to be. It's only the worthless stuff you bury that lasts.

I toss the bottle back in the hole when I'm done, leave a swig for someone else, and take the rest.

When I drop it on her desk over a week later, telling her it's shit anyway, I think she looks surprised that I found it. It takes a while for the dirt to stop pouring out over all her papers. I think she must be in awe because when I sit down in my chair in the cubicle next to hers, I don't hear her singing the same song.

It's "The Boy is Mine" followed by "She Loves You," but it's too slow. She keeps missing the notes.

So I hum along because I'm afraid of what I'll find if I don't.

SHE LOVES ME
LIKE A TAPE RECORDER

I tend to talk to myself, asking life's more important questions. But the odd thing, the thing about my little heated debates that Sara seems to love, is I don't really say a word until I'm asleep. Not until after I tuck myself in and she wraps her legs around me underneath the blankets, not until my heavy-lid eyes close do I really get into it with myself – and lately I've been recording what I say.

And I'm answering my questions. All of them. And the answers are good.

They're so good that I go over to my friend Jordan's house and beg him to listen. He does. He can't believe it. It makes perfect sense what I'm saying. I hit 'play' on my tape recorder and we just can't believe how much I know.

I say to myself, *Lev, why is it that so many people don't wake up early in the morning?*

Jordan hears me groan on the tape and then answer: *Because coffee is better in the afternoon when it's not needed. Because people only wake up early to go places they'd never go if they didn't have to. Because we don't remember our dreams.*

Jordan says, "Hey, ask yourself a question for me, will ya?"

But I'm not sure it works that way.

I tell Jordan I can't explain it, that I just talk in my sleep, ask whatever is on my mind.

"Oh, come on. Give it a try, will ya?" he says.

"I don't know. I was about to take a nap – why don't you ask me then? Why don't you see what happens if you whisper it to me?"

I get comfortable on the couch, and later he leans over into my ear, and he does.

"You see," he whispers, "I got a girl problem. What should I do about this Tiffany I met last week at work?"

What an answer! I didn't record it. Jordan said I should have because I told him exactly what to do – and he did it and it worked even better than could be expected.

Tiffany and Jordan have another date scheduled next week and it's starting to look like marriage – at least, it does to me and Jordan, if you were to ask.

He wants me to help him out again, but I'm not tired.

"Oh, come on. Take a little nap for me," he says. "I want to ask you something."

When I wake up, he looks better than he ever has.

"Did I tell you to wear that?" He smiles and I know I did.

"Let's go out," Jordan says. "I want to try out everything you said."

"But Tiffany," I say.

"Will say 'yes' no matter what," Jordan says with a big grin, giving me a playful slap on the cheek.

At the bar, I see Sara. Her big eyes lock on mine and we're at it – talking, laughing, drinking, asking each other questions about things that don't matter, like 'Do you believe in Santa Claus?' or 'Do you catch July fireflies?' I tell her about the tape recorder and the ability to answer anything I'm asked. "Except it's just in my sleep," I tell her, and she loves me for it. She's wild about it. She says she can't believe I'd tell her something like this to be with her again.

"Just one more night," I start to say, but she stops me.

"It's okay. I don't mind if you talk in your sleep," she tells me, putting her hand on my knee.

"Good," I say, "because I want to tell you something tonight. Something special."

"Only in your sleep," she says with a wink. She doesn't believe me. Not at all. But she loves it anyway.

"Let's try it," she says. "Let's go back to my place. At worst, I'll kick you out."

At Sara's, I sit on her small couch waiting for whiskey sours, for her to place them on the coffee table, for her to wrap her arms around my shoulders, for her to pull me in against her. When she enters from her small kitchen with two drinks in hand, I don't know what to do but smile and say "Ask me something. Ask me anything you'd like to know. Anything at all, but wait 'til I'm asleep."

"Like what?"

"Something only you would know. Something no one else knows," I say, pulling her toward me.

She bites my bottom lip, smiles a little crooked and stares hard at me. She has something in mind, I can tell.

"Something only I know, huh?" she asks.

"Yeah," I say, putting a finger to her lips. "Not yet, though."

And she does.

She waits until after our drinks, after the kiss, after

we've held each other and said the things about future careers in environmental law and traveling to South Africa people like us say to each other, wrapped up on a small Ikea couch. She waits until my eyes close and my head rests on her pillow.

Then she does it – Sara asks me something about herself that not even she knows the answer to. Not yet.

"What was it about?" I ask when the bathroom light hits my face and I see her standing in its doorway.

She doesn't say a word, only takes the tape recorder in with her and closes the door. After a few minutes of muffled sounds, she comes out with last night's makeup running and brings the recorder back into bed with us.

"Did you have me solve world hunger? Bring about peace?"

When we listen to it, wrapped against each other beneath her sheets, she slides her hand into the waist of my pants and unbuttons them. She wants me.

Because I know her better than anyone else.

I know her better than she does.

THIS IS NO TIME FOR WISHING

11:11 – Make a wish

If I can't have Sara marry me on the moon in front of our graduating class, if we'll never walk hand-in-hand under the largest elm tree in the galaxy, then I want her to kiss me once and say "I love you Jeremy. I love you like a wild, hungry dog and I want you to fly me around the world. The moon, too."

But if there's no wish strong enough or right enough or awful enough for that, then I wish she'd at least travel to space with me.

That's what I want.

That's my wish.

12:12 – Wish for the stars

I wish I'd never won that free trip to the moon, two tickets to space.

I wish I'd never gotten on the rocket, that Sara never

turned to me and showed me the craziness beneath her shirt – exposed wires, chemically complicated explosives.

I wish the moment it launched she hadn't said "I think I got you into something bad, Jeremy."

I wish she hadn't grabbed my shoulder and squeezed, saying "I'm going to blow it up. The moon. Set space on fire."

More than that, I want her to never mention Lamar again.

I don't want to hear her say "We're going to be bigger than just you and me. We're going to mean something. You, me, Lamar – we're going to show the world wishing won't change a thing. When they look up into the night and see what's missing, the darkness all around them, they'll know, Jeremy, they'll know. We're going to show them."

I want her to shut the fuck up about Lamar.

And when I say "Can't we just love each other in the glow of the moon?" I wish I never had.

I wish Sara wouldn't apologize, wouldn't use his name. "Sorry, I'm so sorry for getting you into this, Jeremy. Lamar is going to be happy, though. So happy."

It hurts to hear her say that.

There is a pain in my head and it's Lamar. It clouds my vision and makes it hard to want anything other than Sara minus space minus me minus suicide explosions.

If I can't have that, though, if some things just have to happen no matter what, then I wish she never met that fucking Lamar. I wish his radical organization was dead, blown apart into thousands of pieces, tiny bits I'd put in my pocket, the kind of little scraps you'd pull out accidentally with a receipt you shoved in earlier, tiny pieces of paper you'd let scatter in the wind and fall across the sidewalk. I wish Lamar would burn and Sara would come live with me and my mother, safe from Lamar and his fire.

1:11 – *Wish harder*

I wish the city wouldn't resemble Hell so much, that Sara wouldn't cry "Oh my God, what's going on? The world must be ending, Jeremy."

I wish the fire sweeping across the four-lane highways stopped melting the glass skyscrapers, and that Sara wouldn't pound my chest, screaming "Where's Lamar? Is he dead? His brother Trev, he's dead! Jeremy, answer me! What have you done?"

I wish for all that, but if I can't have it, then I wish Sara would come home already and be done with her stupid job forever. She works so much. Her boss, that loudmouth Trev, keeps asking her to go out afterward, to dance, to meet his older brother Lamar – a university guy, an artist with crazy ideas.

Not my Sara.

She comes straight home.

We have coffee together.

We kiss, watch British comedies with my mother.

I wish Sara didn't have to work with Trev.

2:22 – *Keep wishing*

If I can't wish for Sara not to lose her job because I told her boss Trev "Fuck you and your radical shitbag brother. Stay away from her," then I wish I came in with flowers, saying "Sara, I love you, damn it. If you'd just give me a chance I'd buy you a burger. We'd hit it off. We'd love each other like there was nothing better than what we had right then in front of us. You'll see."

If I can't have that, then I wish for fire again.

3:33 – Hope it comes true

I wish Sara could see the moon through the smoke, that she'd wrap me up in her arms, maybe shake me a bit, yell "Jeremy, you have to stop this! You can't get so angry – I barely know you! You can't keep wishing for the same thing over and over. You can't. Take it back."

Of course, if I can't have that, then I still want fire, and if Sara cries "Jeremy, you have to stop! I don't know how you're doing this! You have to stop!" then I wish my mom would meet Sara, that they'd sit down at our kitchen counter and have a cup of coffee, look at pictures of me in my T-ball uniform, the red one I wore before Dad left, before I worked at WonderHill Convenience under Trev and his shitbag brother Lamar.

4:44 – What did you wish for?

I wish Sara and my mom wouldn't hate each other, that they wouldn't argue about where I went wrong. I wish my mother wouldn't insult Sara like that, that Sara wouldn't say "You drove Jeremy's father away, just like you're doing him."

I wish Sara wouldn't run to Lamar's place like that after she fought with my mother, that she wouldn't go there, telling him I'm stupid, boxed-in, that Lamar wouldn't take her in his bed, kiss her neck, tell her how big the world is, that things like me need to change.

If I can't have that, if time won't allow me a loving family, then I wish I were strong enough not to follow Sara to Lamar's shitty apartment, that I'd have the strength not to padlock the bottom gate or pour gasoline over the steps. I wish I wouldn't set that complex on fire and sulk away under the moonlight.

5:55 – Don't tell

I wish no one wanted anything, not even Sara. "Please, Jeremy! What are you doing down there? Get help! Oh God, Jeremy! Oh God!" I wish my mom never spoke, that no one, especially not Sara, wanted anything better than what they already had. That wishes weren't real, that time had no significance, that we were just what we were.

No wishes.

None.

That's what I want.

That's my wish.

5:57 – It'll never come true

I'd really like it if my boss Trev and his brother Lamar would stop teasing me about how I'd like to fuck Lamar's girlfriend Sara, but it's not so bad. They're not so bad. And it's nice when Lamar and his girlfriend Sara come to pick up Trev because Sara, she's the nicest girl I know. When she smiles, it's like I'm flying around the world, landing on the moon, marrying her in front of my entire graduating class. That's what it's like and I'm fine with that, okay with just the feeling.

It'll never happen. That's fine. I'd like it to happen, sure, for Sara to love me, but if I can't have that, then that's okay. I'll clock out at nine, go home to my mother, watch her British comedy, lie about how funny it is. I don't mind because just knowing Sara, seeing her for a second or two, makes it better, makes everything okay, even if that's all it'll ever be – loving her with just my eyes.

That's what it is.

That's my life.

AGAINS

You were the son of God, so sick of Heaven you traveled to New York where you met Simon the Jew.

You were once like him –

Jewish.

You tried to convert back, but your father said no. He sat you down on a cloud and told you a whole religion rested on your shoulders, that it was important you *played the part.*

He had his.

You had yours.

"Just ask the angels," he said before disappearing into a rain cloud.

In New York,

with Simon,

you were an ordinary guy.

You liked him.

"Simon," you said, "call me Jesus the Plain."

And he did.

Except he called you 'the Pain.'

And why not?

It was his lack of belief that made you his friend.

That, and Simon's dickishness. He didn't act like you were the son of God, a god in your own right, a power of allness.

He owed you nothing.

And Simon told you so. "The fuck you're not paying for drinks tonight. I paid last night!"

You didn't even have to trick him into thinking he saved your life, that you were somehow even.

Simon didn't believe,

that's all there was to it,

and in time you stopped believing too.

At a club in Brooklyn, you made out with his girlfriend in a dark bathroom, and when she grasped your back, pulling you into her, "Jesus Christ, fuck me," you did.

And it reminded you of your father.

He'd been asking you "FUCK, THIS IS WHAT YOU SAVED THEM FOR? ARE YOU EVER GOING TO CLEAN UP?"

But your father was a pushover when it came to you, and you avoided the question.

You pumped up the celestial good intention until your father's voice sounded like harps bouncing off clouds. It was an old trick, but a good one. Heaven was full of junkies. But you couldn't be their supplier forever.

In New York, at the club, people danced like Romans around a fire, and the music pounded in your ribs like spears.

Simon told you "It's fine. You can have her."

And that struck you as odd.

He'd never given you anything before, and you liked that about him.

He made you suffer a bit, and it was like old times.

So this?

This was different.

This was off.

But you should've seen it coming.

Or maybe you shouldn't have.

Why would you suspect Simon to lean in and kiss you on the lips?

It didn't bother you.

You believed in love

and loving

and passion

for all.

What bothered you were these Christians, your children of sort. Six of them, all of them — it doesn't matter — young guys, Holy Bible College polos pressed tight to skinny chests.

They stared at you.

They judged you.

The smallest, thick glasses, four drinks an hour, he made to get another vodka and club

and he pushed you.

And

you

fell

into the bar with a thud.

Simon stood.

He defended you.

"Buddy, it's 'Excuse me.'"

And the small one, he ignored you both.

It was an accident, you told yourself.

But you knew better.

And when Simon whispered "He's an ignorant fuck," the small one heard it and he drove his knee into your thigh like a spike into the palm.

He did it hard,

and you crumpled.

Simon stood up.

He helped you to your feet.

You kissed him

on the forehead,

then the lips.

Because you wanted to show the Christians, the gawkers, all of them,

how to love.

"That's disgusting," the small one said.

His eyes flashed.

The music pulsed.

And you felt something.

It was more than anger.

He called you disgusting.

It was something you hadn't felt before.

He hurt you.

You'd always been so forgiving.

He pushed you.

The DJ stopped.

They stopped dancing like Romans around a fire.

"That's just fucking wrong," they whispered.

They stared.

They murmured.

They wanted to shame you.

Simon stepped forward

and spit.

And you, you looked for stones.

The small one, youth pastor on Thursdays, his gold cross exposed on his gold-tan chest, he picked up a bottle

and swung

for the temple.

And you, you thought to sacrifice yourself,

to take the blow

and suffer.

But then you remembered what your father said.

You hated the idea you were like him, but in the end, the thought of these people carrying your name was too much,

so you knocked over your drink.

It poured out,

and you let it

keep

pouring,

like a flood of locusts from a farmer's field,

and you thought, *Why not? Why not locusts?* So locusts it was. They poured out of the glass. They ate the bar wood. They ate the music. They ate Simon and his screams and the college kids and their dreams. They ate up the streets and the lights, the buildings and the night, and you couldn't stop yourself.

You destroyed New York.

And then, after that, it seemed silly to stop,

so you let it rain.

And you knew

you were

your

father's

son.

THAT'S WHAT
YOU TELL YOUR FRIENDS

You'd been watching me work on the car all day. I couldn't get out from underneath. You laughed, and I saw. My brother came over and we drank and later you fell down the steps and broke it. Your wrist hurt so bad you told me "Never touch it again." That's what happened. That's what you tell your friends.

When you witnessed me searching Amazon, unable to spell the word ELECTRIC, you looked away, coughed into your hand, and you dropped my glass on your foot. It smashed and the shards got you. That's what happened. That's what you tell your friends.

You wanted to call your sister Susan. She had the baby. I wanted to call John. He'd called me earlier. Your phone died. You pulled at mine. I let go. It was your fault. It was your hand that hit. It's not even bad, though – looks like a beauty queen's lip, almost pretty. That's what you tell your friends.

You shoveled the entire driveway out. I threw snow in

your face. It wasn't funny when I slipped. It wasn't funny to laugh at me on the ice, pawing at the ground, trying to get up when I was down. I smashed it hard into your shirt, let the snow crush between your breasts.

I locked the door, rummaged through the cabinet, forgot you were out there in the cold because the fall hurt my back, because of the way you laughed. Tell them or the police or the neighbor or your mom or no one at all. Tell them on the hotline I said hello.

And in the summer, your best friend Jane stayed over all day while you worked. My clothes on the floor. I told you she'd been there a few minutes, standing in our bedroom, waiting for you to come home. I dressed in the bathroom. That's what happened.

You stayed out late, forgot to bring cigarettes. Your grandmother's German figurines, the little spoons from fifty states, they fell, bent, broke, whatever you want to hear.

You went through my phone, into my wallet, you moved my keys, you forgot to lock the door, you smirked, you turned the channel, you finished my sentence – you got in a car accident. Nothing that won't heal. It could be worse. You could've died. Maybe you should stay inside, rest. I'm taking care of you.

Tell everyone that.

I'd been drinking all evening, holding your wrist damn tight. I held you to keep my balance, told you "You're not worth what I'm paying." It was a joke.

Leave that part out.

I fell forward, burning myself on the grill, letting you go in the process. The heat hurt. I shot away from the pain, threw myself onto the steak fork you held. The two long steel prongs pierced me, in my kidney, out my spleen.

You were only standing there.
That's what happened.
That's what you'll tell your friends.

WHEN YOU DIE

Dear Wife,

When you die, you'll be so incredibly thin.

It happens that way, I know. Your liver stops working. Your body is a sin. Mine's nothing now. It takes only a strong wind to lift me from my chair.

Like that gust of a woman you call your mother. She picked me up from the kitchen table where I rested, carried me over to the couch.

I could have killed her for that.

If my body would have let me.

You see, honey, when you die, your mouth won't take in what it needs. All the nourishment your body wants will be replaced by drugs the FCA is still only considering.

I said to your mother, "Sue, what are you doing? Put me down."

She looked at me, a crumpled body in her arms, said "Oh, Simon, I'm moving you somewhere more comfortable. Now be quiet and let me do it."

When you die, you're so insulted. Everything stings: in-laws, needles, warm smiles, and hellos.

I know. It happens.

Your parents, friends, family, foes, all of them visit, treat you like you're nothing more than your worst fears — a sniveling child, groping for help, tugging at the coat of anyone near, asking "Please, make me safe for years and years."

But you won't have that. Not even months.

"Sue? Are you here? Someone? What time is it?"

On the couch, after your mother left, I cried because no one was home.

Not our daughter.

"Sara? Honey?"

Not our son.

"Sam? Please, what time is it?"

An empty house sounds the same as a six-foot-deep hole. It scares you — the walls, the lack of people. You hear dirt being thrown on the roof, footsteps walking away in the rain. It makes you crave company.

You'll understand when the time comes, how you sur-round yourself with hugs and hellos, offers of medical marijuana and talk of the weather.

My kids, your kids, they're mad because of the visits. It's not fair, they say, all these people want to see you.

Learn to share.

When you're two feet in the grave, up to the shins, you notice your friends come to say goodbye. They never say it, not to you. So it's "See you soon. Stick in there." It's a light clasp on the back, a call-if-you-need-anything hug.

"Can I give you a hug?"

And while they visit, while you say "Yeah, go ahead, hug me like there's no tomorrow," your friends begin to think it's rude, too, that they're taking you away from what's important. Because time with anyone who is not your family is time you can't hold your daughter against your weak chest.

So when you die, your friends won't be there. Not one.

But you're not alone. Not yet.

Near death, still holding on, you whimper while your better half cries. Those tears are martyr holy water. They're hate drop by drop. And though they pain you at first, you watch them roll, fall off her cheek, the neighbor's nervous laugh, the parade through the kitchen, the talk as if you can't hear them.

"You're so strong to be doing all this," they say.

But not to you.

They don't even whisper when you die.

I know.

And when you cough in the warmest weather like winter's around the corner and your sides are thin metal ribs rusting away, you'll be so close, so incredibly angry at the comments your neighbors make, even if you never hear them, because those are the comments that wake you in the night, make you glare at the person asleep next to you, think *Keep breathing, champ.*

In bed you stare at the ceiling, afraid to close your eyes. You think, *This could be the last time I'm awake.* So you never sleep until it's over. Not until someone shuts your eyes. When you die, you're too afraid it'll be the last time you see anything at all, so you never close them.

Never.

Instead, you stand in the doorway of your daughter's room, stare at Sara like she's a holy ghost underneath a white linen shroud, her purity blanketed, protected, until a thief in the night, who you won't be there to stop, lies, steals it away along with her panties.

When you gulp air like a fish dying on the beach, there's another reason your eyes stay wide open. Because if you can't watch from Heaven, you know you won't see a thing.

And besides, if you shut them you see the attorney fees, car accidents, Sam's fistfight, Sara's wedding, your better half in bed with the neighbor.

Either way – closed, opened – when you die, you'll be as quiet as a

spouse

parent

friend.

One hundred dollars won't save you from the cancer you contract from the sun. Because your death doesn't believe in materialism. It's the quiet, simple things in life it takes from you, like your children sleeping and strawberry ice cream.

It's soundless when you die. I know. You won't make a squeak, not across Sam's floorboards after you kiss him goodnight, not when you shut Sara's door, because when it happens, you go to without a word. You sit in your family room and you don't watch TV. There in the dark, you think, *What kind of mess is this? Shouldn't I end it, go back upstairs, tell the person sharing my bed I can't?*

And without the lights on, really, it's like your eyes are closed anyway. Seems like there's nothing left to do. And that's how you do it.

That's the secret.

When you die, you do nothing at all. When the lungs quit, the heart no longer measures time. When nothing counts, nothing happens. You don't live.

You die.

WHEN YOU'RE DEAD

Dear Simon,

When you're dead, I'll come into your house, collect your things in a burlap sack, and tell your wife you never loved her. I won't even jimmy the window because – you know why. She leaves it open, undoes the lock. Just for me.

Gayle loves me, Simon.

Every Sunday night.

While you attend midnight vigils, grasp at life like it's an old lover and plan whether you ought to let your brother speak at your service, I'm waiting in the woods behind the pine trees, creeping on the edge of your little piece of property.

I'm there watching for Gayle's signal – a bathroom light, on and off again.

Because when it's over, when you're dead, buried beneath a drooping sycamore, inside an expensive pine wood box lined with cheap ruffled silk, there is no vigil for you to attend, Simon.

There's nothing.

Nothing left.

Nothing except

the biggest ceremony of all.

Your funeral is my birthday. That wondrous occasion will be preceded by a viewing that will go long into the night, and I won't be there.

Neither will Gayle. She'll leave early, excuse herself because of the sadness and come home to your house where I'll be waiting. I'll take her grief, wrap it up in my alive arms and help her with a jar of peaches. I'll twist the lid right off, something you could never do. She'll cry, say "Do you think it's wrong? Am I awful?"

She'll cry because of you, but more so because of the children. "What'll they do?" she'll ask me. "Do you think they'll look to me now to be the good one? The one with all the answers?"

I hold her tight for you, look her hard in her soft, wet eyes.

"He was a saint to them, you know," she'll say. "Christ, I can't do this."

I'll let her cry. All night. Against my chest.

She wants to get on with her life, Simon – as terrible as that is.

So, I'll tell her "That's not wrong, love, to want to live."

That's true, isn't it, Simon? It's not really *that* terrible, is it? To want that?

And do you know, Simon, what I'll be putting in my burlap sack while she continues to cry, standing there in your bedroom?

You do, don't you?

Memories. The ones of you and your mother.

Memories of trips to Ocean City with your kids. That picture of you holding Sam above your head. Even the one where you look like you're not paying attention at Sara's dance recital.

I'll be putting you in there, into my bag, all the way to the tippy top.

I'll tie it closed, swing it over my head, let it land in the back seat of my Lexus, right on the black leather seats where Gayle loves to makeout because it feels like hundreds of dollars, my hand on her thigh. Because it feels like the last two years, my lips on her neck. Because it feels like being alive.

When you're dead, I'll tell Gayle, "It's no problem, love. I'll put this all in storage until you're ready. It's hard to know what to do with this kind of stuff."

I'll ask her for the security code, as if I didn't already have it written down on a cocktail receipt in my wallet.

On my way to the storage garage, I'll stop at the bridge, let the bag drop, plop into the water, listen to the splash like a farmer does after he throws his burlap sack of unwanted puppies into the cool water of his favorite swimming pond.

Just like that, Simon.

And in the storage unit, I'll take what's good enough to keep, try on your watches, that two-button blazer, the navy one you used to wear in college when Gayle was still attracted to you.

It fits me – like your house, your wife, your kids.

It fits me so well.

When you're dead, delivered to a hole in the ground by your brother and his two sons because little Sam and Sara are too young to carry your heavy weight, don't wait for her. Not your wife, not Gayle. Don't leave any room for her to be dropped down beside you for the rest of eternity.

It's not going to happen. She didn't mean that promise. Not that one.

When you're dead, Simon, when you're beneath a marble stone marker stating how long you lived and who you were at one time, I'll drive back to where I left her, re-introduce myself to your kids, say "I'm a close friend of the family." I'll sleep there for the first time, right after your oldest closes her eyes.

And in the morning, I'll be there for Sam's eggs and toast.

And that next night, after that first dark day you're gone, I'll re-introduce myself again, this time as an even *closer* family friend, a close, close friend of their mother's. I'll sit next to them on the sofa, inches away from their legs.

When you're dead, Simon, I'll come inside. I'll sit in your house and be everything you never knew I could be for Gayle, for Sara, for Sam – for me, so alive and willing to be you.

Now that you're gone.

Now that you're not you.

Now that I don't have to be me.

REALISM IN SMILES

This artist I know keeps trying to paint himself as a really happy guy, but, without a doubt, it looks fake. The smile droops and the eyes show nine-to-five. It's awful. Ruins it every time.

But last week, Jordan, he walks into my flat and tells me he sold one.

"Sold one what?" I ask him, because what the fuck.

"I sold a painting of me," he says.

"No, not one of those ones where you look almost fucking happy. You couldn't have."

"Well, yeah, one of those, and the buyer turned out to be this big shot art critic from New York."

I stare at Jordan's half-smile as he explains that the guy, like a manic drug dealer, enjoys discovering the next big thing to get his hot fix, and that this guy came stumbling down 5th and Race after a bad hit and just happened to stare up at my friend's awful apartment window and see it – a portrait of my friend nearly happy, almost even enjoying himself.

So I ask him, "Jordan, how do you feel, huh? Like a million bucks? Like a big shot?"

"No, like maybe I should paint myself again."

And he does.

Jordan goes home and locks himself in his studio and paints himself over and over again. And all the while, his portraits, they're selling like the next big thing.

At auction people go nuts. Something about the truth of it all and a humble honesty like honey in the veins of Mona Lisa. That's what they say when they fork over what I couldn't make even if I sold my honest-to-God smile, my actual lips and teeth, to that perv doctor down on Gerald Drive who offers us gold and dope dreams.

And now, overnight, this artist I know, Jordan, he becomes famous for his unhappiness. He's done it. He's the next big thing. And he goes in his studio to paint and paint and paint, and he tries and tries and tries to make the brushstrokes look happy, to make his smile a drop of honey, but my friend Jordan, the artist, he settles on a landscape painting instead.

"Landscapes don't have to be anything," he says to me. "They're just there, happy or not."

Jordan, my painter friend, he can't help it though, and he paints himself in, a few strokes, and there he is right on the bank of the Rhine River.

And although he's really happy with his career now, even with his landscape painting, the little self portrait of him, the one standing on the bank, well, it still looks fake.

"How can you tell?" he asks.

"I just can," I say.

"Yeah, me too. Didn't know if I should say anything."

"Don't," I say, and he gives me that fake smile like things are okay even though the landscape is ruined.

GOING TO KILL A BUFFALO

Ned Harper had never seen a buffalo. He'd never watched one run. He wanted to. He wanted to see one tonight.

Ned Harper had never been so impulsive before, had never driven farther than Pittsburgh. Philadelphia to Pittsburgh. Once.

Now, six days after telling no one, after just leaving, Ned sat on the hood of his car, staring up at the Wyoming stars. "I like it here. I like here a lot," he said. It was the first time Ned had spoken aloud in over a week.

At work no one spoke to Ned because at work Ned sat alone. There, he was the last of a small IT department.

Here, in Wyoming, beneath the stars, with the buffalo coming, Ned was something else – surrounded, maybe.

Ned pulled the fur blanket around him tighter and waited.

Before Wyoming, Ned hadn't been waiting for anything. Not for Anthony. Not for him to come down to IT. Anthony from PR, he'd waited. He had told Ned so. Ned remembered. Anthony had stood alongside a prairie, had waited two hours to snap a photo. Ned had just listened. At least that was what Ned remembered. Ned couldn't always remember when he spoke. Before Anthony, not one other person had come down to IT that month.

Only e-mail. No one talked. Almost always e-mail. Ned couldn't always remember.

It was pretty easy for him not to speak. On the road, it was even easier.

Ned really did want to see a buffalo. Maybe in the morning, he thought, if not tonight. Although tonight would be great because Ned Harper had never wanted anything so much before.

He relaxed his hands behind his head and felt his eyes get too heavy for him to see much at all. "In the morning," Ned forced himself to say aloud. It troubled him to hear his voice, to not quite recognize himself. His voice sounded off. It wasn't Ned that he heard. It was wind and tree branches breaking, bouncing off a distant canyon wall like thunder over a poor Midwest stable.

He sounded wrong and it made him smile.

He thought about trying to say something else. He had to be sure it was him speaking. There had to be some last remnant of Ned Harper in him somewhere, the man who'd left work, gotten into his car, and had begun driving across the country.

When all he heard was drums and chanting, Ned felt ready.

It had been the first time anyone had come down to his department in weeks. It had taken Ned a few seconds to separate Anthony from his e-mails. He'd stared at him for a while before turning his gaze back to his dark monitor screen. He hadn't been sure why Anthony had been talking to him, but felt as if Anthony were trying to explain something terribly important to him.

"Yeah, Lewis and Clark saw it firsthand. The Indians would take a buffalo skin, I mean the head and all, with the horns and all that heavy fur. The thing must've weighed a ton. But they would take it and wear it over themselves and run with the buffalo. They would run them right to a cliff. They'd start a charge toward it and lead them right off."

"What happened to the Indian?" Ned had asked.

"The Indian jumped out of the way or onto an outcropping or something, but that's how they killed buffalo."

Ned had stopped typing his e-mail. He wasn't sure when. He just sat there and listened to Anthony, listened to the buffalo falling. Without much thought, he had shut down his computer, pressing the button on the tower until the click had told him it was over. The screen went dark. It had already been dark.

Anthony had asked him something.

"Have you ever seen one? A real buffalo?"

Ned had barely noticed being asked a question. His powerless black screen seemed so much more interesting than all the e-mails he had ever read or written in the last eight years of his employment. He could see them, the buffalo, falling right there on his monitor, could even count the carcasses piling up at the bottom.

Ned didn't answer Anthony, not even on the way out the door.

Ned couldn't speak then. Not yet. He had been staring too long into monitors to make words.

The thunder brought him back. Ned heard it all around him. Could feel it moving through him.

He could feel the sound as he sat up on the hood of his small brown Civic hatchback. The thunder became a more clear pounding. Ned knew he had done the right thing staying in the park after hours.

Only stars and him, and soon them.

Hundreds of them.

Ned grinned.

The pounding thunder was coming.

He still had time.

He was ready.

His car was parked less than a mile off the road and less than a mile from where the Grand Teton National Park map told him not to be, where *absolutely* not to be, where the herd would make their way from one mountain valley to the next.

Ned knew he was ready as he got behind the wheel of his Civic and waited, listening to the growing thunder coming toward him. It was a mountain of sound in the darkness that seemed bigger than the Tetons themselves.

Did buffalo always move like this, he wondered, like a sweeping rain from one valley to the next?

Ned didn't finish his thought. They were on him, a force flooding past him and around him, then right into his car – into him. They were in it together now, something worth waiting for, something more.

The impact and thunder almost prevented Ned from becoming a part of it. His hand trembled with the key, flipped the ignition, turned on the lights, his foot fell on the gas.

Ned had never before seen a buffalo and was not let down by the massive mashing of brown bodies folding in on him and his car. He was not let down by the hooves that moved him, Ned Harper, IT Department, and his

small economy car forward, onward, together, his headlights dancing across the plain, leading the charge.

WHY THE WOLVES
TAKE THE CALVES FIRST

She should've been the one.

From atop my horse, I scanned the mountainside, sweeping my eyes over the herd of cattle navigating down its bend.

If Mother Earth had a son, he'd be named Montana. She'd watch over him, never let anything bad happen.

But it would anyway.

Watching the last head of cattle, a small steer, become part of the moving train, I'm reminded of the missing calf from last night. His mother weighed eight times as much as him, moved slower.

It never seems right.

The wolves come down the mountain. They separate the herd, and they take the calf every time.

You never see it, only imagine how they do it.

Except when I play it out in my mind, it's not always the calf they take. It's her.

Even if it never really is.

The torn ground where the herd spent the night – the trampled grass, the blood – it tells me what happened.

The small hoofprints stop. From the looks of it, the wolves dragged the calf the rest of the way, pulled him off his feet. The imprint of the poor thing's body across the mud looks like it goes on for some five more yards. The mess of blood, it's an easy enough trail to follow. No point in arriving at its end.

The wolves are somewhere on the mountain, somewhere between the very bottom and the very top. I'm somewhere between that, between a herd of free roaming beef and them, so I reload my rifle because it makes me feel better.

Somewhere else, between all of this, is my wife Sue.

When I wipe my leather glove across the mud-caked denim of my work jeans, the calf's blood smears.

No point in staying clean. Sue'll know.

Should've sold the mother. Now she won't eat because her calf's gone. Should've sent her off with the last order. Would have if Sue hadn't been convinced that time spent with the mother would guarantee the calf's success on the mountain.

She was wrong.

Shouldn't have bothered trying to keep a calf anyway. Not our business.

We make a living raising free-range cattle. Beef rich from the green Montana grasses they feed on. Our card says so.

It isn't Chicago.

It isn't a life either of us expected. Not at this point.

The costumes fit, though, and the work keeps us busy. I put on the boots, ride the mountain. I wear what I'm supposed to. I keep doing it, all that I can, what I can, keep my mind away from cities, whatever memories lurk there. No more Chicago.

This – I hope it can be enough. It needs to be. Enough to make us smile once in a while when the weather seems nice or the sun dips down behind the mountains.

A redefining of tranquility, even if it's never peace.

The calf's dried blood on my leg reminds me of the crushed red stone in the Montana quarry we passed when we first drove from Chicago to the ranch, when we rode in silence because Sue didn't say a word to me the whole drive.

The red in those open mountain veins looked so natural and deep. It's easy to mistake it.

I need to get off my horse, back in a car before I forget how to tell the difference between quarry dust and blood.

How natural it all seems here in Montana.

The herd has moved on. Maybe to put space between them and what happened last night, maybe to eat.

A deep wrinkle forms on Sue's brow at the news.

I don't want to tell her it was one of the two calves, and I don't have to. She knows.

The loss makes her face twist and show something. What it is depends on how well you know her. Whatever it is on her face disappears as quickly as it surfaced.

Where does she bury it?

Does it matter?

"Well, that makes three," Sue says, sitting down at the kitchen table, pulling out her yellow legal pad.

"It does."

"We'll have to replace our loss and make up the difference by selling higher. Fatten them up."

"Hard to fatten up free-range beef, Sue."

"Well, they'll have to range longer. Maybe go up along the northern side more."

"Can't. The wolves."

"The Jonsons do it."

"Yeah, the Jonsons sent the wolves our way."

"They're managing because they stay out there – camping, keeping an eye on their property. Protecting it."

"Sue, do you think any other Montana rancher who loses a calf to a wolf would begin protecting his livestock by sleeping with them up in the hills?"

My wife stands up, stares at me. She thinks it's my fault, that I can't protect them.

"It's not possible, Sue. You know that. If wolves want one, they're gonna get it."

"The Jonsons stop 'em." Her eyes refuse to meet mine.

"Yeah, and they do a much different business than we do. They raise calves. Their whole world is calves and making them into something the rest of us can decide what to do with."

I sit down at the table, wrap my hands around Sue's.

"We decided to sell free-range beef. That's steers and heifers. The occasional calf is something we can handle. It happens. But we're better off selling that last one to the Jonsons."

"No. We're not selling it to the Jonsons and losing a good investment. It's a natural gain. And you want to throw that money away on the basis that it won't survive here on our ranch." She flings her words. Her eyes are wet.

I understand.

"Alright. There's no reason we should throw away good money. It's our good fortune to have a calf. Free money, right?"

"Why don't you take the rifle up there, Mark? Just see if you can find them."

"I'll try." Something flashes across her face with my last word.

"They've got a den somewhere on the north side," Sue says, "where the pines get thick. I know it."

Trotting off in the distance, disappearing farther up the mountain, the wolves melt one after the other into the tree line, leaving her behind.

I check my rifle, pick up my binoculars.

We packed up our small Chicago apartment. We tried downsizing to a smaller one, one room, but it wasn't enough. We left. It was better than a divorce.

We didn't save any of his things. No boxes full of toys. Possible hand-me-downs. A friend came, took everything while we checked out the ranch.

We moved.

I lined her up. Put my finger on the trigger. She pushed her muzzle back and forth over her meal, not finished eating.

I almost shot. Refocused to be sure of the kill.

I was wrong.

The wolf rested her muzzle on her dead pup. Then on another. She licked and nudged their small paws. Her entire litter. Three little pups. One moved, vomited, was still again.

I put down the rifle.

With my binoculars, I watched the wolf brush her nose over the last dead pup, holding it there until there was nothing left to do.

She melted into the forest away from the den. I

would've left it at that, but she came back to stand over them, nuzzling and waiting.

I picked up my rifle, aimed, and shot.

There was no way I could've known it'd be the last time I'd see him. They told me, reassured us, it wasn't our fault he was taken. It wasn't Sue's.

"Don't look so upset, Mark."

"It's illegal."

"Well, what if it is? There are plenty of other ways you're allowed to kill them."

"Poison, Sue?"

"Yeah, and we're safer for it. We can keep the calf. I took care of it."

"Just the cubs."

"What?"

"The cubs got to it first, I suppose."

"What? How?"

"Did you put it by the den? That would do it, Sue."

"The others?"

"Out hunting or too smart."

"The mother?"

"Can't be around all the time."

"Oh my God, she's still alive?"

"No."

DREAM GIRL

Next to Sara I dream of having tea with a familiar red-headed woman. We sit in her college apartment and talk about a little pond on campus. "It's beautiful and cold," she says. I drink my tea and agree, although the water is warmer than she believes.

It's not a bad dream, just odd to meet my wife here. She seems different, like when I met her for the first time and we both knew we were going to date. Which is strange because I'd forgotten that.

The second dream we skip right to the sex. We're in her old college apartment again, the kitchen, a little place, tight, hardly any room, and I make her claw my back – but in the dream, at the same time while I'm making love to my wife, Sara sleeps through the whole thing. Next to me. She just lies there on same kitchen counter, sleeping next to us while my wife kisses me hard.

Later, when Sara and I go to dinner, to Stacy's on the Waterfront, I'm looking for my wife, as if she might be real to me again, real enough to be sitting there waiting for me, maybe to surprise me with a flip of her hair. I'm looking for her because of guilt, that and because now I remember her car from the dream. The Jetta. That seems wrong. Not the kind of car. That I remember *that* car.

At dinner, I drink wine with Sara until I remember more from the night before.

My wife pulled up to our apartment in the dream, stepped out of her old Jetta, and I got into the driver's seat.

Sara, from the right now, orders clams in a white wine sauce in addition to her glass of Pinot Grigio.

"That's so much white wine," I laugh and say because she's young and cute.

That night, after dinner, in my dream, my wife eats clams too, and I realize I'm superimposing Sara on her.

"I'm sorry, Dream Girl," I say to my wife as she cries and licks the inside of a clam shell.

"Aww, that's sweet," my wife says, "you called me Dream Girl."

We make eyes at each other across the table. Dream Girl orders white wine too. She has to.

Because of Sara.

"Stop superimposing your evening on me!" Dream Girl yells, splashing Pinot onto my shirt. "I hate Pinot. You know that."

As I wipe off my shirt, I stand up in our college apartment and walk toward the door. "I'm leaving you," I say.

"Why?"

"I can't remember."

"I guess you are then," my wife says and disappears, leaving me in a tiny Mexican restaurant that used to be our favorite. In the dream, the yellow music, orange walls make me want to drink too much, kiss too much. I like it. A young woman's back is to me. She stands at the bar. It's Sara, I think.

"Sit back down. You're overreacting." Dream Girl says to me, stopping me from walking over.

"You came back," I say.

"You made me."

"I can't," I say. "This, we, this is good. I love you. We should stop."

"You're making no sense," Dream Girl says. "Why don't you turn right at the stop sign."

In the dream, I turn my wife's old Jetta right. It's difficult because I'm also sitting on a small Ikea sofa in our tiny college apartment making out with her, my left hand on her breast, my coat stuck underneath me, restricting my arm.

"We loved winter," Dream Girl says.

Outside of the college apartment, the snow falls, and I have to turn on the windshield wipers to see.

"We did love the winter," I say and pull my long brown coat around me. "It's cold outside."

"Like the water in the pond," my wife says.

"No, it's not that cold," I tell her with a sad smile.

Inside the tiny college apartment, I'm soaked from falling in the pond. We stopped the Jetta there, outsmarting campus security. We sat at the edge. When we kissed, I fell in. That really happened. In the dream. In real life. A long time ago.

"Stay here tonight. C'mon. I want you to," she says, but only in the dream.

And in the dream, the Ikea sofa feels like warm sex, but when Dream Girl says to stay, I know it's me making her, so I put on my wet jacket to leave, which, once again, makes it difficult to turn the Jetta's steering wheel.

"Where are you taking me?" I ask.

Dream Girl smiles. "I'm not taking you anywhere."

I kiss her neck, drag my lips across the soft skin there, bring them to her ear. Kiss her there. And there.

"Do you still love me?" I ask.

My wife answers. "It's Sara, isn't it? Are you confusing me for her or the other way around?"

I wake up.

My wife wants to know "Whose fucking keys are these? Is this why we're getting a divorce?"

Later, in my car, driving to Sara's, there's a hairbrush on the floor, passenger side. It doesn't belong to me. It's Dream Girl's and it hurts to see because her red hair lingers between the bristles. I pick it up. Out the window the brush flies, drifting over two lanes to bounce against the curb not far from the campus pond we never really moved away from.

This is it, I think as I pull my car into the driveway of an apartment I know – but not from my dreams.

At night there, when I sleep, Sara says, "Wake up, you're dreaming, you're calling me her name again."

Next to Sara in bed, I wonder before falling back asleep if it's a different dream here, if it's the wrong one or the right one.

I tell Sara I'm sorry, that "I love you, you're my dream girl."

"Don't call me that," Sara says, "not yet. I love you. But don't call me anything like that, not at least until you move out."

"Okay, alright, wake me up when I do."

SEEDS OF DOUBT

My Chia Pet stared at me. It looked annoyed, upset at my inability to grow. It can't see me, I know, but still – it looked right at me.

When Craig gave me the Chia Pet still in its box, even then I had the feeling that somewhere inside, bouncing around the clay shell, there was a god watching me.

I brought it home, followed instructions. Now water, now seeds, now water, now grow.

I watched it. *Simon, I'm a little god – your new god – and I have great power. Worship me and tell others,* it said.

I called my therapist, booked a double session, asked about my meds, side effects to sunlight, followed instructtions. Now pill, now water, now mind, now voices, nothing and sleep.

With the green sprouts came more demands. *Simon, carry me above your head and proclaim to others that I am here for them to worship. Simon, water me. Simon, denounce all other religions. Simon, carry me to the window. Simon, do not eat any of my fallen seeds.*

I worried that I had let my mental illness take over my life again, that I'd be homeless and hearing voices for another year. It kept me awake at night, preventing me from breaking the cycle. Now sleeplessness, now paranoia, now missed appointments, now late for work.

At the office, they noticed. My hands were covered in fertilizer. Craig asked me if I could hang around and talk. I left early when I went to the bathroom. I rolled up my sleeves so they wouldn't get wet. My arms looked green. I wasn't sure and it was hot. My sleeplessness was causing delusions and I knew that my Chia Pet wouldn't be happy.

At home I washed my arms again and splashed fertilizer on my face. It smelled and made me sick, but I was careful not to vomit on my Chia Pet. *Simon, I need a sacrifice to be sure you love me. Soak me in your cat's blood and I'll bestow upon you my miracles.*

I'm not doing that. That's crazy. That's not me. I'm not like that. I don't do things like that. I make sense. I take my pills.

Now I swallow, now I'm fine. Now I'm not.

That night, I killed Oliver and squeezed him over my Chia Pet and checked myself into a hospital the next morning.

Simon the non-believer.

They took my clothes and scrubbed me, covered me with a bed sheet, made me sleep. I tried not to notice my arms, whether they were green.

Simon.

The doctors came and I tried to make words. They checked the windows, called security. The room filled with them. They didn't understand. They picked me up. They put me down. They said I left my Chia Pet behind, washed their hands.

I thought about my instructions. About prayer. *Now a believer, now in my likeness, now punished, where no one worships the only god.*

SO BRIGHT
WE QUIT OUR SHADOWS

On the first day, we noticed the beach seemed brighter. Not hotter, only more painful to look at. Sara said, "It's going to be a scorcher today."

But it wasn't.

Off the sand, on the first day, it wasn't much better. We had to make decisions, decide quickly what we needed to see. The gold wedding band on my wife's finger? Was it worth the pain of the glare? The six-inch step before our feet? Painful spots would follow. Sara's wink? We had to consider. We had to know – was it worth seeing, worth the blindness that followed? A glance at the curb cost us. A look to see who stood behind made us wince. It was a little unreal, so we laughed. Sara bought ice cream. I looked at her face, noticed freckles.

On the second day, Sara shielded her eyes, said, "It's getting hotter."

"Not really. It's something else," I told her, "like there aren't enough clouds."

We argued, got off the beach, took our towels in our hands, wrapped them around our heads, made hoods to protect the eyes. Beeping came from the street. Drivers parked where they stopped, left vehicles on the road. They walked to shelter. Indoors, emergency loudspeakers warned: "The glare is dangerous. Ocean County recommends all residents stay inside until the phenomenon has passed."

We wore hoods, saw what we could, kept the blinds pulled. Sara said, "If you close your eyes, it's not so bad." With our eyes shut, the sun came through the lids and brought spots, little flashes of bright, uncontrollable color, fireworks of the mind. It wasn't long until closing our eyes didn't matter, until it didn't stop the sun from blinding us. It wasn't long until the loudspeakers announced: "Sunglasses are mandatory." It wasn't long.

Because it was bright.

It wasn't long.

At least we had the night then.

On the fourth day, people stopped going outside. Sunglasses were no longer enough. The light came through the leaves and we started to fear it might come through the walls. People stayed inside, waited for answers. Science said "Beats me" and we waited for it to get worse. When it did, it wasn't what we expected. Sara said, "Wake up! I can't see! It's coming through the ceiling. It's coming through the ceiling. It's coming."

"Shut up! Shut up! Shut up!" But it didn't matter. Yelling at Sara did nothing to stop it, the light. We felt our way down to the basement, to where we hid underneath the bricked floor of our kitchen, a stone ceiling above us keeping the sun away.

"Will it come through? Will it shine all the way down

here?" Sara asked.

On the sixth day, beneath the brick of the kitchen floor, we huddled in the basement. I stared at Sara, touched the dark outline of her figure. We wished for a brighter lightbulb, thought of the irony, and wondered how long we'd have electricity, if it would matter.

On the last day, everything washed out beneath the sun's glare. No shadows, dark outlines, or edges. When we peeked out from whatever stone, steel, cement enclosure we hid under, the brightness glared, blinded, washed it all out in a whiteness so bright we looked away, held our hands to our faces, covered our eyes, cried until we turned back to the darkness, praying for night.

On the last day, I thought about the previous night, about what I should have seen, what we should have done within the range of a sixty-watt bulb.

On the last day, I walked past Sara toward the stairwell of our basement, the steps once carpeted planks of cedar now a single column of light pouring through a basement door. I stared at the purity of the beam. The light struck against the floor, shining onto the dirt of the Earth, not through the core, not out the other side — not yet. I thought about whether or not there would be night, about how long until the glare came through the rock, until it went straight through to the other side, until there was nothing to stop it, until there was no night.

I walked into the brightness, stepped into where the sun lived. It whitewashed everything with its beams. I turned, saw Sara standing beneath the stone mortar of our kitchen floor. I watched her in the dark there, watched the streams of concentrated light begin to poke through over her blond head. Her freckles now dots of light sprinkled over her, through her, gone. The sunlight went through the stone above her, penetrating. I stood in it, called over to her.

"Is it coming through me?" I asked.

After that we stopped counting. After that we stopped caring. We quit thinking about the days or what we saw. When the sun came through, it came through us. It took days. It took color. It took the night. It was so bright; Sara cried somewhere.

PIECES OF
MY JUNKYARD FATHER

My first pup was a junkyard dog Pop brought home from work.

"Here you go, boy. Take this shit, make sure he don't mess the house."

He'd gone to a great length getting me a junkyard dog. Pop salvaged scrap, located parts from locals. It was nice of him to think of me, to find me what I needed – kind, even, to pick the parts, to put it all together. For Pop to salvage me up a pup, it was love – had to be, considering he'd other things to do, to search for, more important things to find, like maybe my mother.

People came by. They'd drive their brokenness over, dying American pickups, gutted German Beetles coming down long roads. They'd spin their wheels on loose gravel, gun the mountain driveway, stop at the porch. They'd bang at the torn-to-fuck screen door, ask Pop if he knew where a thing was for their beat-to-shit cars, if he'd seen Mom, if she hadn't shown up yet. Pop would put his hands in his pockets, wiggle them in old denim, tell them "Fuck off, Jimmy. I ain't at work 'til I'm at work. Find your own fucking parts."

"No need to get angry, Steve. Your boy's watching."

"The fuck if he is. He's seen worse than grease monkey trash collectors having it out over a thing or two. Ain't that right, son?"

And for the most part, Pop found what they needed, made it so they'd fix what was broken. Old rusted junkers running like new. Family four-door sedans, three wheels now four.

Again and again.

What wasn't whole, Pop made it so it was.

Not everything. Some things Pop couldn't fix, no matter how much he spit, spun the wheels.

Pop's junkyard extended to the backyard. People knew it. If they couldn't afford the county junkyard, they'd knock on the back door, cheaper alternative – like knocking on the oak of my father's rusty-hinged heart. Mom hated it, couldn't stand stacks of tires, axle mazes, playground mufflers. Spit on cars, scratched hoods, rubbed mud – nothing she did slated her thirst, her anger for having to live with us. She left.

Then it really was a junkyard. We really were broken.

I remember that red hair, her yelling like thunder, a storm of broken whiskey bottles popping with glass bangs. Pop's favorite junkers damaged on the outside all because of her. A whole lot of hot noise. I remember. Not her face. Not that.

Pop pissed her off. He'd grab an alternator cap for Mr. Wilgin's '88 Deville, a horn for Petey Smith's pregnant girlfriend's Pontiac.

A missing headlight.

A broken fender.

Pop mended it. All he could.

And it drove her crazy.

The day she left, Pop was at the yard. Mom said, "Wyatt, your father is an idiot. Why he never charges these people what he ought to, I'll never understand." I cried in the kitchen waiting for her to come back, to open my can of SpaghettiOs. Pop found me in the kitchen when he came home, standing there in my little boy underwear, the ones covered in green dinosaurs. I was still holding the can of SpaghettiOs.

I am still holding a can of SpaghettiOs.

Mom?

She never understood, not like me, that what Pop did at work, he did at home, that he had to. When you're good at what you do, you bring it everywhere, you bring it home. I got Pop's smile, what made him tick, understood why he carried springs home in his pocket, gasket caps in his hat. I understood. Mostly after my dog died.

Before my junkyard dog, I'd figured Pop thought only of potatoes. He'd eat them when he'd get home, stand at the sink, peel, not say a word, drop one, two into a pot, let the water boil, stare at the steam, not say a word, look at my cans of SpaghettiOs on the shelf, take one down, hold it in his hand, stare, run his finger along the sealed-shut lid, look at me, cry.

"It's all I want," he'd say. "It's all I need: boiled potatoes, you, me – we're all we need. That's all we need."

He'd eat, sometimes without a fork, bits of potato falling onto him, into his beard. His beard growing. The dark circles under his eyes forming. His hands. He'd never wipe them across his oiled-stained shirt, the pale blue collar covered in dirt, kept clean from what he could. In case. He didn't want her thinking he'd given up.

He didn't want her to come back only to leave me – not because of him.

Not again. Not to me. He'd keep himself clean.

That day, when he dropped my pup down, a plop of metal gears onto the floor in front of me, Pop lied. "They didn't want this lying around the transmissions yard, and I sure as Hell didn't want it. Thought you'd might. Remember about the house. No messes." After he'd said it, that was that. He'd given me the world on a platter, told me not to crash it into Mars. He'd almost walked away. "You don't like it, get rid of him." A nervousness, a gruff not used to trying. Pop didn't know if I'd notice his effort, that he was awake, aware I was there.

If I didn't like the thing, get rid of it? Who was he kidding? I loved it, every part, every piece, my junkyard dog.

He knew. Pop knew. Must've. He turned back to say something else, saw me with my new friend, me smiling a dirt tooth grin. "Thanks, Pop. Thanks. He's awesome."

I wrapped my hands around my pup's thick, hard neck, smelled rust, the dirt of the yard, kept holding him. I held that dog all night, thinking I'd everything a boy needed. That, and because I was afraid to let go.

Didn't take long 'til I'd pissed Pop off good asking stupid questions. "Do you think Mom'll like him?" He'd started in on his potatoes, no chance to pour salt, no reason to answer.

I'd eaten a can of SpaghettiOs. Pop told me to. "If you don't eat the whole can, I'll lock you outside."

"I'll tell."

"Who?"

Guess it didn't matter as long as I ate the whole can.

Before my pup, I used to ask about her. Too much. "Pop, is she coming back? Do you think she'll like the haircut you gave me? Pop, you think she'll notice I can open my own cans now? She will, won't she?"

Before my junkyard dog, Pop would get mad. "Don't ask stupid questions!" he'd yell, smashing his plate, slamming his hand, punching the stove. That last one made it hard to eat for a week. Had to rig a propane tank. Didn't really care, though.

I fed my junkyard dog what he wanted, needed to eat. That was more than you'd imagine. Pieces of aluminum, tin, sometimes lead if I could find it. That pup, he ate anything I found. All I'd do was pull out the screwdriver and there he was, mouth open, and I made sure he ate every bolt, every screw went down the hatch.

That pile of rust, my first pup, he left oil all over the house. Couldn't help it. I'd clean it up, hug him tight, roll him around, oil where necessary, leave him tied to an old car, pretend I had to save him, that we were captured or lost. In the backyard, plenty of places to hide, I found what I was looking for; that junkyard dog, he was always where I left him.

Pop reached out to me bringing that mutt home, scrapping him together like that. I should've known. Never knew a good thing until it was gone. Mom? Pop didn't want another mouth to open cans for. He didn't want another someone to take poor care of, but I'd cried cold all winter, telling him a dog would keep me warm. He'd liked me since I was born. He was a bit broken, wanted to try. It wasn't hard.

"A good pup, he'd make sure I eat every day."

"Why would a pup help you eat? You haven't ever trained a pup. Don't know shit about raising a young thing. How 'bout something you can't fuck up?"

I was stubborn, knew a thing. "A pup is hungry like me, Pop. If I had a pup, I'd eat whatever was in front of me or else."

"How do I know you wouldn't go soft? How do I know you wouldn't feed a pup your own food?"

"I wouldn't. Besides, if I don't eat what's in front of me, he'll gobble it down. Like Mom would. Like she'd always do." He hit me hard then. I wasn't wrong. He knew it, but it wasn't something he could really admit to. Not then, not with me.

Still, he didn't trust me, liked to believe I wasn't hardened by my mother's leaving, that I was soft. Considering what I did for that dog, he was right. Getting me the kind of pup he did, an old junker, was the right decision for a boy who couldn't handle losing anything else, the best thing for a father who could only put together the pieces of some things, of only what he could.

My pup, my junkyard dog, he was only a month old when he got hit by Mrs. O'Hanlon's pickup.

I tried to save him.

Everyone said, "You're crazy. What's wrong with you?"

Pop understood. "He's fine. What the fuck's wrong with you? You going to let your stuff get smashed? Idiot."

The neighbor boys, the O'Hanlons, they said my dog wasn't a dog at all, just useless junk, bits of cars, old coffee cans, springs.

That hurt.

"That's not true! You're both dumb 'cause of your mother."

The O'Hanlons would get annoyed. I'd always blame their mother's drinking for their stupidity. This time, they heard enough, let me have it. "Our mom's not as much a drunk as your own."

"My mother's not."

"The Hell she's not! Why'd she up and leave you and your dad then?"

"My mother's not a drunk."

They seemed honestly confused by this. "Whenever our mother leaves, it's 'cause she drank everything we hid or because Dad's supposed to be in town."

"Well, that's not the fucking case."

I didn't like the O'Hanlons. I punched the oldest in the face, let my fist crack against the hard part of his jaw, his blood on my shirt. The O'Hanlons busted my lip, as expected, blood on the yard, pain in our faces. All expected. All part of where we grew up.

My father, my dog, my country blood – they all bled the same, which wasn't unusual for where I'd been raised. All that oil and rust, all over the grass, polluting deep into the earth's core, infecting the drinking water – that blood was dangerous. And I didn't even notice it was mine.

Pop did, and he was pissed, which I get.

The thing about Pop was he could smell blood better than a hound. Any time I'd scratch myself on the old elm, get into a whipping fight with the Weeping Willow branches, he knew. "Wyatt, come here! What's that on your arm? Were you fighting with switches? Was it the O'Hanlons? Those Irish fucks, they hurt you?"

I'd have to calm him down, hope he didn't notice my

rusty shirt.

You don't understand your father until you've become him. By that time most fathers are estranged or dead. Unless you have a bullshit relationship with your kid, a healthy one, the kind where you bring home a Golden Retriever, talk about your day at work. A good father throws you to the wolves. A good father buys you one.

Which reminds me of how I ended up looking like I'd been mauled.

That July afternoon, Pop told me "Get that goddamn thing out of the house." He noticed when things weren't given the love they deserved. He noticed my rust-stained shirts. He noticed the way I woke up crying, thinking I was still in the kitchen with a can I couldn't open, a mom who wouldn't come when I called. He noticed, like when he got home from work and I wasn't there playing in the abandoned cars out back. He noticed the broken parts of my pup in the street, the blood there, all rust, my blood, all wet. He noticed Mrs. O'Hanlon's scribbled note about rushing me to town. He noticed and drove to the county doctor, slugged him in the face when the doc said he'd have me removed for neglect.

Pop held me then the same way I held my first pup. I didn't notice at the time the doc holding his chin, watching us from a safe distance.

Sure that mutt was old parts Pop threw together. Sure, I loved those parts, the tins cans, the wheels. I smiled when I saw the red tin of my pup's Folgers coffee can belly. I whistled when I pulled his Goodyear tire paws forward and onward with a bit of old rope used as a leash. Sure, they were parts for me to play with, parts that made up my dog, the first thing I'd owned and knew would never run away. Sure, Pop was one part, I was the other – our family, the best we could do. He was the best dog we could take care of. Pop showed me how to fix his injured front paws, patching the rubber, how to mend his wounded hind legs, greasing the swollen rear axles.

Those parts, my first pup, they escaped me on the hill of my mountain driveway. I'd dropped the leash, couldn't keep up. I ran. My speeding mutt, he was well-oiled. On the road, heading to town because she'd heard her husband might be at the Salvation Army hostel sleeping it off, Mrs. O'Hanlon blared music, wiped away tears, pedaled the gas.

I ran. My pup sped forward onto the road. Mrs. O'Hanlon's truck screeched, slammed hard on its breaks, kicked gravel. My arms stretched. Its Ford fender crushed my pup's Folgers coffee can belly. I ran faster. My hands touched a paw. They grabbed a timing belt tail. My junkyard dog, those parts, those pieces, sailed around me with metal whelps. I felt a fender. And she, Mrs. O'Hanlon, she came to a stop.

My father, Pop, he picked up the pieces after the doctor's office, after the punch to the chin, the police, the misunderstandings, the standings. He built me a new dog. Christmas he introduced me to Ms. Sara Wells. He bought me a real hound who I named Junk.

He cried and held me that morning. "What did you call him? Say that again."

STAINS

Sam rinsed his coffee cup, not bothering to stare down at its persistent dirtiness. Long ago he learned to throw in the towel when an impossible stain presented itself. He thought more people should accept the stains found at the bottoms of mugs. Just because something bothers you, Sam thought, doesn't mean you need to eliminate it.

Sam wished more often than not, that other people would accept that sometimes things weren't perfect. He shook his head, thinking of his colleagues taking lunch, chomping away on their cucumber and avocado sandwiches, discussing the new improvements they'd made to their lives.

He brought his attention back to the coffee. The dripping began. For Sam, it was the best part of the morning. He stared at the coffee maker, letting it lull him into a trance. He was neither here nor there. With each splashing drop, Sam considered life. It was harsh of him, thinking people crazy for scrubbing a stain. Especially, Sam thought, because at one point in his life, he'd have attacked that dirt lingering at the bottom of his mug with the vigor of a handsome Latin dancer stealing some tourist's wife.

Sara's little poodle Go-go bit Sam's ankle, breaking his trance, ruining his favorite part of the morning.

"Fuck you, Go-go."

Sam realized he sounded like an eight-year-old.

"I hate you and hope you die."

He stared down at the dog.

It was the size of his foot, puffier. He didn't like Go-go, mainly because he couldn't see his eyes.

"Are you looking at me? Is that your ass? You fucking disgrace."

Go-go's ball of fur body stared at him or maybe the door.

"Why can't you just go through the fucking doggy door I made you?"

He looked at his back door, stared at the magnetic vinyl flap at the bottom. He'd spent an entire weekend traveling back and forth from Home Depot working on that door, that medium-sized dog door.

It'd been on sale.

"It's too heavy for Go-go," his wife Sara had said.

She'd informed Sam the day he'd finished the project. It still bothered him – a three-hundred-dollar hole located at the bottom of his door.

He imagined a skunk coming through it, raping Go-go, leaving before anyone could do anything about it.

"Go-go, you slow shit. Go outside. Stop staring at the fucking door like it's a goddamn portal."

Sam decided if his morning rants were caught on tape he'd be divorced, in which case Sam would have to sneak through that very dog door to kill Go-go.

It would have to be done.

Before Go-go, Sam used his morning time alone to think about stupid stuff like the brown film staining his coffee cup. Other times he sat in his favorite chair and read. It didn't matter. It was his time.

It used to be, at least.

"Children would make me happy," Sam had told his wife.

"We have Go-go," she said.

Sam left at 6:30 every morning, which, from the moment he woke up until he left for work, gave him two hours to get ready and be alone.

To do whatever he wanted. He'd loved that.

This morning, using the banister for support, Sam jumped down the last four steps to the bottom of his stairwell and heard the sickening snap, the squish, the muffled yelp reverberating beneath his weight.

Go-go.

In one quick jump, Sam shattered everything he loved about his mornings. Soon his wife would come downstairs, talk to him, cry. He'd never have a second cup of coffee.

Sam lifted his weight off of the broken remains of his wife's cherished teacup poodle.

The fur did not bustle up into a mound of annoying life as it should have. It did not make high-pitched sounds, and Sam couldn't help but notice that it didn't bleed.

Thank God, Sam thought. *I broke the neck.*

No mess. Wife still asleep.

Sam leaned down, scooped up the small, crushed ball of fur, and darted to the front door.

Sam knew what he'd tell his wife. Go-go had been digging at their fence lately. He must have gotten out underneath it. He thought about the posters he'd have to put up, the time spent looking for Go-go.

Damn it, he thought.

Through the window, Sam watched his neighbor's car warm up across the street.

With Go-go in hand, Sam stepped outside.

He scrambled across the street, ducking down until he was behind his neighbor's sedan.

He was pretty sure his name was Craig. They'd talked a few times. Maybe it was Chris. No, it was definitely Craig.

Sorry, Craig.

Sam dropped the bundle of Go-go behind the back tire.

Still warm, Sam thought, as he took a sip of his coffee and walked over to his car, keys in hand.

He was gone before his neighbor Craig put his key in the ignition. Gone before Craig cried and knocked on his front door.

When he received the call from his wife, he agreed it was terrible news and left work early.

Sara needed him.

Later, he handed her his mug, watched her shaking hands hold it for warmth.

Sam held her then, gazed affectionately as she drank the hot tea from the mug's stained inside.

"I can't believe him," Sara said.

Sam shook his head in disgust.

"He killed him," Sam's wife whimpered.

"Yes, love, he did, and I hope he has to look at that stain on his driveway for the rest of his life."

A BUCKS DEVIL
AND THE COUNTY GHOST

In Bucks County, the house I used to live in, it's haunted. The ghost there looks remarkably like me, but I'm not dead and it's not my father. It's not my mother. It's not my sister. It's not Grandma Ruth or even cousin Ted, all dead, but nowhere close to me or my old house.

I'm not haunted by them. I'm not anything by them.

Ha.

There's just one ghost in that house, and it looks even more scared than me.

Ha.

It materializes through doors and surprises you.

"Hello, can I help you?" it asks as if it weren't dead, weren't scaring you to high Heaven. What's funny is that the ghost, it comes through the door so you have nowhere to go.

Ha.

I had a girlfriend once who saw the ghost float right through the bedroom door – then everything went black.

She smacked face-first right into the wall, running the opposite direction.

That made me smile – the ghost, always coming through the door. You had nowhere to go but into a wall or underneath the bed or into a closet. The ghost made you a shivering mess, and I like a cold, scared, shivering mess.

Ha.

I got him, the ghost. I understood his fetish – hated him for it. It was sick, right, but it was kind of awesome, that sort of power, to be able to scare anyone, make them climb walls they couldn't climb.

They were frightened. All of them.

I wanted that.

But I didn't want to die. I didn't want to be some pathetic ghost. I hate ghosts. I hate spirits. They remind me of my father and your friend. They're like my dead family, always there but not there, scaring you, probably watching.

I can hear them laughing, the ghosts.

I want to take their thin souls, run them over my teeth. I want to scare them over and over 'til they want to die. I want the ghosts of your loved ones to run through walls. I want the dead that haunts your house to shriek into the sunlight, to burst into pain – anything to get away from me because I don't want to hear any laughing other than my own.

I want the spirits floating around in your attic to be so afraid of me that they'll crawl away, disappear into sha-dows. I want to eat the ghosts in your basement, strangle the demons in your trees. I want to be the darkest thing in the alley.

So I've started to practice.

I make faces in the mirror where my eyes don't look right, where my whole entire face seems like it belongs to someone else. It's capable of anything it wants, my face. The twisted lips, sneered shut grins, eyes stretched with hate. The faces I make in the mirror are the faces you hope you never see.

They've changed me.

I'm not the same after seeing what I can look like.

I suppose it unhinges the soul a bit, to see yourself, to know you're the most dangerous thing in the room.

Ha.

I took out a tooth from my jaw, watched myself do it in the mirror. I swallowed it, told myself it would grow back.

Ha.

I read books on demons, witchcraft, Satan. I find myself rereading *Paradise Lost*, thinking I can rule them all.

Ha.

I don't want to sacrifice women or slit a goat's throat. I want to swallow down the spirits of bad angels, take my hand and hurt ghosts with it.

And I'm at the point where the only thing stopping me from doing so is nothing at all.

So I've started.

I'm doing what I want.

Do you understand?

When the ghost who used to live in my old house came terrorizing through my door, I was ready. I charged right at him with one of my new faces, reached for his throat. I probably looked like some sort of mad dog or one of those terrible new fast zombies. Whatever I looked like, my house ghost flew back through the door, letting me smack against it, scratching like I could already taste what was left of his soul in my mouth.

He was scared, my ghost,

and I loved it,
even the splinters
underneath my nails.

SOUNDS, GLORIOUS

When it sounded like a helicopter spinning in the room next to you, you didn't say a word because by that time you felt it too – and it made you think of your father.

"What?" you asked.

"The sound, it's more of a vibration, right?" your friend Mason speculated about the low humming coming from you.

You pounded your third beer down and said, "Yeah, it feels like someone crashed his car into a giant tuning fork right next to my fucking head. I can't stand it."

And you couldn't.

The sound had taken over in the last few days and most people had already left the base, but you lived there with the sound for over a week because it was home. You'd been stationed where your father raised you, and when you repeated your jumbled ideas again to Mason, he asked "What?" because he didn't understand or couldn't hear or didn't think or something like that.

It was confusing.

All of it.

On account of the sound.

"I don't know," you said to Mason. "I can't stand him."

"I don't know either," Mason said because he had no idea you were talking about your father, because he had no idea your father was the source or that you carried it too.

And it wasn't just you who knew your father returned from the desert humming louder and louder until officers more important than you found his remains and secreted them away to investigate – to see how it spread.

It wasn't just you who cared.

Lots of angry people on the military base stood pissed and confused because a painful vibration pulsed through their brains.

It had started in an office – a laboratory, actually. Scientists playing with chemicals hoping to find new energy or a better bomb. They dropped a formula, matter mixed with matter. They did it on purpose. From a safe distance. Farther away from where they tested any of the others even.

And nothing happened.

The chemicals, unstable molecules engineered from scratch in a lab, didn't react, so with protective gear on, the scientists occupied the testing zone, studied their work, a perfect waste of intelligent danger and disruptive design. Thick gloves disposed of the project, which really wasn't anything much at all. "This is silly," one scientist, your father, had remarked. He'd picked up one of the two metal liter bottles that had originally housed the mixing compound and stared at it. Absolutely no reaction, he'd thought. Then he'd thought of you, at home, on the base –

a military brat turned foot soldier, a scientist's unwilling son. Your father placed the cylinder into a protective case to bring back to the lab until he could be positive no harmful toxins had been released in the project's obvious failure.

To him, later, when he rode in his open jeep across the desert back to the lab with the wind against his suit of rubber, it all seemed so unnecessary. The precautions, his hi-tech rubber coat, the extra-long clean up – all of it for nothing. It hadn't worked. This, he'd thought, staring down at his gloved hands, this is for insurance purposes only – but inside his gloves he'd felt a tingle, and that was the sound, the start, the beginning of the pulse vibrating through you.

Your father thought the tingle was his mind's way of saying let's discard these awful military safety gloves, let's see the living tissue of our bare, naked hands and be far away from science and be done with proposed technology for new bombs and wars. Your father, he wanted to be home. He wanted you far away from failed experiments, and even farther away from successful ones. He loved you, wished you hadn't enlisted, and was positive that if he released the safety latch underneath his protective rubber helmet, he'd be fine.

He'd have heard the sound, though, if he had done it – and he would've realized it came from him.

Instead he kept the rubber suit on and felt it through the gloves, through the fingers, and later you. It was the start of some ripple effect, and when you learn of this you're surprised he didn't feel it in the cylinder from the very start, that there wasn't already some sort of vibration humming at ground zero.

But you're not a scientist. And the cylinder wasn't the

cause. If it were that easy, you and your friend Mason could finish your beers, break into your father's lab where he kept things like old metal cylinders and memories and you could hold it, the cylinder – smash it even, crush that horrible container of unstable molecules underneath the heavy steel leg of an examining table. If you were like your father, you'd figure out an easy solution for obliterating the sound that caused so much discomfort to those you love. If you were like your father, you'd make it so you'd never have to listen to that low rumble humming through you. You'd destroy the source like he did using basic physics, a military base roof, and the concrete street below.

But it's not that easy. Your father tried explaining that. To you. To everyone.

Your dad couldn't think, so he held his head, stayed later, farther away. He couldn't concentrate. The dissonance. The sound. It reverberated a never-ending failure you could feel in his touch.

In the end, he couldn't think of you. He just couldn't think. No one could who came near him. The few times he'd stopped by, your father had opened the car door, allowing the sound no restrictions, so you felt it more, heard it louder. Without the car acting as a barrier, people, your friends, they ran at him, yelled at you, called over the noise, "Will it stop?" They grabbed your father's shoulders. "Have you figured out what's making the sound?" They pushed him away, shoving his chest hard. "What is it, Dr. Rulik? When is it going to stop?"

"What?" your father had asked them.

"The sound, the hum – what is it? It hurts."

"It's me."

With the sound vibrating through the barracks and humming through the streets, it wasn't too surprising, only ironic maybe, that your father, the source of it all, became quieter, more physical in his frustration, speaking less and seeking an end.

And in the end, to get your attention, he yelled, only to remember you couldn't hear him, that you were crying like you did when you were still a little boy, holding your head, pressing palms against your ears.

In the end, you didn't have to say it was his fault – he felt it.

And you felt it too, because it spread from him to you, and when Mason asked "Are you going out there in the dark?" you told him to wait in the car before you started your walk into the desert, happy that the last thing you'd hear would be the same sound as your father.

SETTING YOU FREE
IS THE BEST THING I'VE DONE

"I'm not trying to be rude," Sara says, "but setting this bird free is probably the best thing you can do right now." She smiles, touches my still-bandaged hand.

"The thing flew into my car. I'm caring for it," I say without looking away from the cage. "Besides, it's not ready to be released back into the wild so it can die some miserable death."

"God, you would say that. You really think this thing needs you."

Behind the wire of the cage, the injured owl closes his eyes, refusing to look at me.

I understand why.

He doesn't respect me.

Although he likes the attic, enjoys the cold, the easy meals. Which is stupid, Sara says, when I mention it.

"Why?" I ask.

"This owl loves being in a fucking cage? That's ridiculous."

"Why's that?" I ask because I want to know what's so ridiculous about someone caring for you.

The owl opens his eyes, not because he wants to see me. He hears what I'm doing.

"Are you going to keep feeding it rats? How much are they?"

Sara taps the little cage I've extracted the owl's lunch from. She stares from the rat to me, back and forth, like she can't decide what's worse.

"Until I set him free," I say, dropping the rat through the wire door that sections off my attic into a makeshift owl home. "And they're free. My father dropped them off earlier today."

I throw food in front of the rat, figuring it should have a last meal.

The owl stares at the white rodent sniffing around the floor. He is anything but fast and more or less plops down on the rat from his perch, like a rock falling on someone's head.

"You really need to let it go," Sara says, coming up from behind to wrap her arms around me.

"I feel like I've put so much into him," I say. "I want to make sure he makes it when I set him free. It'd be a crime if he has to go through the whole healing process again."

"What did your dad say when he came over?" Sara asks.

"Him? He only wanted to know if I followed his directions."

"Did you?"

"Yeah. I'm just not fond of his methods. It always seems like he doesn't care about the animals. He's rough."

"Your dad wouldn't be a vet if he didn't care." Sara

unwraps her arms from me to make sure I can see her know-it-all smirk.

"Yeah, well, you're still a dad or a husband even if you don't like your kids or your wife. You can still be a vet if you don't like animals," I say.

"Why do you have to be so negative?" Sara asks. "Your father didn't do anything wrong."

"He didn't do anything at all. He should've kept on with her."

I imagine I'm my owl.

"Can't you let that go too?"

She says it with spite, and I know who she's talking about. I know she means it, I just don't know why.

Outside, in the headlights, we see a narrow forest, the long line of light illuminating the dark where I imagine wolves wait.

Sara says I'm afraid of my own shadow, that the dark here is nothing scarier than what's locked in the pet carrier.

But really, it is dark here.

And really, my owl wants safety, not this.

"Wait 'til you see him fly away without even looking back," Sara says.

"Can't wait," I say, already thinking this is a terrible idea, that this is one more thing I let people push me into because I'm weak-spirited. Taking care of this owl has been the best thing – the only thing – I've done on my own I'm proud of since I don't know when.

Except that's a lie.

I know when.

Since my father moved out and my mother's new boyfriend broke his arm in an unreported accident I never got in trouble for.

This has been the best thing since then.

"Take the blanket off the cage," Sara tells me. "It's so dark he won't be afraid. Don't let him get spooked by the headlights, though."

She says this as if I have no idea what my owl likes, as if I haven't taken care of him. Sara undoes the latch, opening the carrier so I can watch my owl disappear into the forest.

But he doesn't move.

Not a wing.

Injured or not, there's no attempt on his part to fly into the blackness, to understand what's out there.

And I appreciate that.

I like him for it the same way I like not talking about how I feel, what I want, or where I should go now that I've finished college.

So I close the carrier door.

"I'm not sure I should set him free yet," I say.

"Then why did you drive all the way out here?" Sara asks, staring at me like I'm the one who should be left in the dark.

It's a good question, though. The answer is probably a mix of things, but mainly my spinelessness and her being a terrible bitch.

"I don't know," I say. "I have no idea why."

FUTURE PERFECT

In the future, when you die in a video game, there's no coming back. That was my doing. I did that. And I'm not sorry.

If it upsets you, that's a good thing. It's important for you to get upset. It means you're human. In the future, that's more important than ever.

Because things can get blurry. They were for me.

They've gone to great lengths to fix the blurry parts. In the future, things are clearer. Because, in the future, when your character dies after he gets shot, he fucking dies. It's like having one quarter.

Before I was born there were arcades where you could pump machines full of your money. You never paid more than you were worth. That's something. That's why I can't even compare it to that. Because, even then, if you had a quarter, it probably entitled you to at least something like three lives – three chances to do something epic.

My grandfather told me that once. He cried the whole

time too. Told me how he blew up an entire alien base once and slaughtered a city of zombies. Now he never completes the first level because he's afraid to die. Sometimes he doesn't even start the game. He only watches the intro with the sound all the way up.

In the future, my grandfather hates his real job. He wishes it were more epic than estimating monthly revenues. Sometimes he types his name into the Player One Database and acts like he forgot his ID. He's hoping they'll let him on, as if he were some young Dominic Dillianhaul from Nebraska who has never played the game before, as if he were someone different and new.

Someone other than himself.

They know the trick: One game, one life – that's all you get. All you need is proper ID to start. Then you can play the game, Dominic Dillianhaul.

My grandfather, along with most of population, doesn't have the money to spend on a new game. There was this one that got released the other day called *Dimes and Dames*, a first-person futuristic cowboy adventure where you basically are just about the most badass hero I've ever seen. I thought about it, looked at the price, and decided that an education and maybe my first home weren't worth it. In the future, games cost more than you might think you're worth.

My grandfather and the rest of America used to hope someone would die quick and sell his game. But it doesn't work that way anymore.

I took that one away, too.

I'm supposed to be sorry about that. So, sorry. If it offends you, you should seek help.

In the future, it's like going on an organ donor list. You have to wait and have a reason. Why do you deserve to play Simon DeFinch's *Gales and Ruin II* game? What? You just want to see what it's like compared to your own? I'm sorry, sir, but your application has been denied.

Used games are reserved for those with broken or defunct ones, games where they didn't even have a chance to begin, to really start. Shit, that must be depressing. Just starting and BAM – the game console turns red and the game shuts off or something won't move or your character can only walk, never jump.

My cousin had a son who couldn't use his kidneys. He must have felt like a broken game. The boy next door, the one in the wheelchair, I wonder if he feels that way too. I wonder if he plays.

In the future, once you lose, it's over. The game can never be used again. In South Dakota, a kid's military pursuit character jumped off a ledge because most of his friends' characters in the game were dead. There was no more point. He hasn't been able to get a new game yet, and so the police finally promised him one, anything to get the kid off the roof. His parents won't let him play, though.

Why would they after what happened to me?

In the future, some guy who played with the same pack of wackos who had managed not to die for some six long gaming years, he gunned down his entire group during a Sunday night mission. Not the people, the characters. The game version selves.

But in the future, that's the same thing.

They're suing that guy, one couple who was part of the group. They're pressing charges, claiming he can't feel, that he's dangerous to anyone in or out of the game.

I never liked them anyway, though.

In the future, that guy will have a whole lot of nasty charges pressed against him. It'll be a landmark case. It's the whole point of the laws, after all – respect for death, for life, for adventure, for greater deeds and my grand-father.

I'd shoot them again, though, but I'm not getting another game anytime soon. And neither are you.

A NEW RELIGION
FOR FATHERLESS SONS

My father not in Heaven.

This is the first line of my new prayer. It begins and ends there, right where my father wakes up during the funeral service, falls out of his casket, coughs, and stares at me.

It begins there because it didn't end there like it should have.

My father is still alive. He died three years ago from stage four Lymphoma. It was awful – he really fought it, though, from Heaven and back.

When he fell out of his coffin, I cried like life was crazy, hid under my chair and prayed – *Please don't let this be a dream.*

It took one night for me to change that prayer – *Please don't let this be real.*

I couldn't decide what I wanted more, my father alive or my father back from the dead. They seemed like two very different things, because one is not the other. Because one entails a media circus, questions about life, people at your door, praying to you, asking for guidance, if maybe you couldn't heal their feet or the cancer in their eyes. One is a whole lot of Hell and the other is just something sad kids pray about.

The media was everywhere, along with people in droves. They swarmed my tiny house. A spotlight shined through the window in case my father woke up and somehow ended world hunger by kissing my forehead goodnight.

The TV news slept out front.

The sick and dying slept out back.

My father ate cereal and communed with God in the bathroom. Behind the door, the entire room was filled with water and fish. I opened it and stared into the ocean, trying to eavesdrop or maybe see Him until I realized God wanted nothing to do with me, so I slammed the door shut.

He wasn't ready to talk to me then.

Now he's afraid to.

Outside, on my front lawn, they asked, "Is it true? Are you the son of God?"

"No. You want my father. He's not his son, though."

"What?"

"He's not God's son. He just met the guy, that's all."

"What about your mother?"

"She's dead."

"Is she coming back, too?"

"I don't know and neither do you. No one does."

"What about your father or God?"

"I'd ask them, but they're swimming in the sea right now."

"Holy shit," they'd say, and push past me so they might talk with my all-knowing father.

The truth was, though, that my father didn't know everything.

He just knew the one thing no one else did.

He was the only guy outside of the *Bible* to ever come back from the dead.

Just my father.

And later me.

It's the one question we all have in common: What is there after life?

Everyone wants to know.

Just like they did then.

The people camped in my yard and asked the same thing, wanted the same thing, needed the same thing – hallelujah. They wanted my dad to tell them they were right, that their pastors told the truth.

"Excuse me, kid. If your father doesn't mind, do you think he could just explain what's good, what's bad, and, more importantly, whether it matters at all?"

"Oh, and be sure to ask him what's after death. Get details."

"Sure thing, sir, consider it done. I'll make sure to ask my pops what happens if you follow every rule in every book about everything God."

Those people, those vagrant souls followed every move my father made. They wanted him to be their savior, their peace and purpose in life.

But I wasn't sure then, and I'm not now, that my father was really what they needed.

He wasn't the same.

Death changed Dad. Because maybe death was death even if you woke back up.

When I asked my father about the afterlife, he smiled and

told me that God wanted us to be his family and that we were in for some trouble.

That same night someone threw a torch on our roof, and someone else did too. Another person threw something through my window. There was so much smoke I thought for sure I wouldn't have to ask about the afterlife ever again.

But when the smoke cleared and we were secured in a nice hotel with armed guards, I did. "What's waiting for me in death, Dad?"

"Nothing," he said.

"What?" I asked.

"There's nothing waiting for *you*. We'll die alright, but our little family isn't going to Heaven. Not like the others. Not to stay."

I swallowed hard and stared at my father, realizing I'd been damned out of blissed eternity.

"I can't go to Heaven?" I asked.

"We're God's family for a reason," he said. "You can see it, but never have it. It's not for us, son. We have a job to do. A calling."

"Dad?"

"He wants us to suffer like you can't imagine, son. To show others how."

"To show them?" I asked, but in my mind, my dark little mind, I already knew I wanted something else.

"We're going to, too," said my father. "We're going to show the world what it means to suffer and still love someone so great."

He took me by the shoulders, looked at me with the biggest smile, and it burned me when he said "We're going to tell them what we see, son, about the reward that's waiting for them."

Maybe it was those particular words. Maybe not. But my father's blind explanation of what lay ahead of me, the staggering weight of those words, crushed my soul and cast me down. It sent me to my knees.

But I wasn't praying.

Kneeling there on the hotel floor, fists full of cheap carpet, a sense of hate washed over my skin, now hot, now burning, now red with annoyance.

And instead of comforting me, my dear old dad threw open the blinds and told the crowd of people outside what he had told me: "We're going to show you the way."

But I had a different idea of where to.

He lifted me to my feet, brought me to the window. I thought, *He wants me to wave.* He pulled out a 9mm, shot me point blank.

He did it to show the others how it worked, how we were to suffer, not them.

He did it to put a bullet through my skull to explain to the world how I would come back.

He did it so I would tell them how beautiful it was.

He did it for me to wake up and rejoice, to praise the other side and say "It's as real as the grass beneath your feet, people. All you have to do is work for it."

But I lied instead.

I didn't hear the bullets come through window, the ones from the government-issued rifles. I didn't hear the screaming or the helicopters in the air. Not a thing. Not even my father's bones splintering as he was taken down by sharpshooters stationed across the street.

I was dead.

Then I wasn't.

And I lied about what I saw.

I heard the gasps when we stood up, brushing the glass

off our clothes.

I heard my father say "This is what it means to be loved."

I heard the people applaud.

I watched their smiling faces, the happiness found in my healed head, in my father's words, and I knew I wanted to take that away.

So I told them what they always wanted to hear whether they knew it or not.

"There's nothing after this. You're nothing. I'm nothing. My father is a liar. Your father too. Like the priest and shaman who told you never to swear."

It's been three years since I've seen my father, since we've parted ways and I became the fatherless son of an entire people. They call me The Truth-Bearer, and I smile and wave.

"The man I once called my father," I tell them, "was misguided. He wanted to give you something to believe in, and, in doing so, caged you, causing only misery and pain."

"Thank you," they chant.

"You're free," I tell them.

Three years and I'm not sure what he looks like anymore.

Three years and on TV they show him with a beard.

But I know that's not him.

They've locked him away, taken his kidney to see what happens.

They'll probably try his heart next.

And who can blame them?

No one believes my father like they believe me.

They think we're scientific anomalies, that he lied and I'm the truth.

He's probably below the White House.

Hell, I'm not sure I could even see him if I wanted to, but then again they might let me because a whole lot of people believe in me now.

So many I could tear the world apart.

Because I told them "This is it. There's nothing beyond. The sea in my bathroom? That's something my father had me tell reporters. I'm nothing like him. You've got to believe me."

And they do.

It's what they always wanted to hear — that they've been scammed.

I tell them what my father told me: "There's nothing waiting for you."

And it frees them

to do what they want.

They believe. Because, like my father, I'm the only one who knows, the only one who's waking back up.

And when I do, I tell everyone the same thing: "Nothing. It was nothing and it'll be nothing for you."

The naked mashing bodies in front of me, the spilled blood, all of it rejoices and howls when I announce "There are no rules to live by, no God to abide by. There is only today."

Gunshots and screams. A celebration of my words.

Tears and flames. Loved ones thrown away.

I tell them to hoist me up on their shoulders and just how black it's going to be when they die. How scary the nothingness is that awaits them.

"Let me be your guide," I say.

And when the non-believers shoot me with their high-powered rifles from faraway buildings, screaming "Damn him! He's the devil! Don't listen to that boy!" I smile in

Hell, surrounded by my new believers who never seem surprised to see me, standing above them on my fiery mountain.

"Don't worry," I tell them. "I won't tell a soul."

CASTING

Jonathan stared at the back of his mother's head, noticed gray streaks, thought he ought to do something about those when she slept. He liked to help when he could, practicing the words, the hand gestures, what he'd read under his covers the night before – because it made his mother happy, because Jonathan suspected it was what his father would have done for her. And Jonathan's older brothers, Simon and Arthur, caused more trouble than anything else, so he had to study extra hard, to murmur extra long to help her. Because if Jonathan's father were alive, he'd make things better for her. It'd be like magic.

But he wasn't.

And Jonathan, the youngest, most like his father in the most important ways, found himself left to pick up the slack, to heft the heavy tomb from the basement, to hide *The Difference* under his bed, dusting off its pages, memorizing the more important passages, the ones meant for adults like his father, the ones about blood and sacrifice.

Jonathan didn't mind, even wished he could help more – like right now.

The pickup truck in the opposing lane crossed the solid white line for the third time in only a few seconds. It sped down the hill, approaching the small maroon van Jonathan's mother drove. Jonathan watched his mother place her palm against the plump midsection of the steering wheel, watched her wrestle with whether honking would be necessary or rude. Jonathan knew if he didn't do what he had to do, his mother and two brothers would die. The steering column Jonathan's mother rested her palm against would fail to deploy its airbag, become a blunt spear, crush her chest, crack her ribs, rib would puncture lung, blood pouring where oxygen should. No final words. The impact, its force, Simon's neck – snap. Arthur's head against the dashboard, smack at the nose, hemorrhage, the gulp of uncomfortable blood down the throat. Death.

Jonathan closed his eyes, remembered his father, his ability to see what could be, the future, their conversation about being different, being the change you wanted to be, the cost, the words, *The Difference*.

Like magic, Jonathan opened his eyes, slowed time, understood the new future he'd created and whispered something to his dead father like "Is this what you were talking about?"

Jonathan's mom began to press her palm harder against the soft vinyl, emitting a slight beep at the oncoming pickup truck.

Jonathan watched the current future, envisioned it, how he'd survive, how the door would break his left wrist, how his mother's door would absorb the impact, her headrest bruising him underneath the eye, so Jonathan did what he had to – he picked up the bottle of water at his feet, thought of his father, unscrewed the cap, imagined his dead father's book *The Difference* in the basement, saw the words he wanted, the ones under the "Use Only if You Love Them" heading. Jonathan read them to himself, repeated the incantation, chanted the words backwards in his mind. He bit his bottom lip, spit his blood into the bottle to complete the spell, tossed the glowing water out his mother's open window, watched it splash against the pickup, felt the future change. The pickup's steel fender tore into the side of his mother's small family van. Jonathan felt the metal bite his ribs, bones pierce his heart, heart sputter, thoughts flutter – the magic worked.

THE LAST MEAL OF MR. CLAREWATER

"Hurry up and eat it," said the small, roundish man. He wore muddy denim overalls patched with fabric torn from old T-shirts, and his red-rimmed eyes seemed out of focus. It was as if he were staring at something other than the large, filthy man in front of him.

"I can't. I can't eat another bite."

The small roundish man picked up the wooden spoon that sat on the broken table. He handed the larger man the spoon and eyed the window. "Hurry up and eat it. They'll be here soon and there will be nothing I can do to stop them."

The larger man, seated as he was, began to shift his weight in his chair. Any semblance of comfort taken in this action was stripped away by the small roundish man's utterance of 'them,' the very proclamation of which had been enough to make the larger man stop his shifting and begin to cry.

"Mr. Clarewater, please lock the door. Why won't you

even try?"

Mr. Clarewater wouldn't lock the door. He wouldn't barricade it with a dresser or the now useless refrigerator. He wouldn't do any of those things because he had listened to the radio.

Mr. Clarewater told the larger man tied to the chair in front of him a simple no. He told the larger man this because Mr. Clarewater understood that he was as good as dead, plain and simple – unless.

The unless of the situation was Johnny Nishmann, the large man uncomfortably seated in front of Mr. Clarewater. Johnny Nishmann, who had been wandering from home to home, eating whatever he could find before the 'they' from the radio came and took it.

Johnny had heard the radio, too. It was more dumb luck than anything, but when Johnny was over at the lake, he'd found one that still had some juice. The message came over loud and clear: They were coming. No point in hiding your essentials; put them outside your door – your generators, your gas, your rifles, your fishing tackles, and, of course, your food.

All of it.

Put it all outside in a nice pile and they wouldn't come inside. If they had to come in, they would – and then they'd get you, too. So, put everything outside the door because they're on their way now and it won't be long.

Johnny had put down the radio, clicked it off, and ran. If he were going to live out the winter with nothing but what he already had in his belly, Johnny figured he'd better have a lot in there.

So Johnny – not the smartest man, but a survivor nonetheless – began eating.

Houses left years ago, houses left months ago, houses

with people still in them, anywhere that had food outside the door or in a forgotten basement, Johnny went.

He ate his way through suburban neighborhoods and out into the fields surrounding them. He ate his way past the fields and into farmers' very backyards. He ate his way through their storage shacks, through their pantry sheds, through their back doors if they were open. He ate their beans, their cabbage, their roots, their berries. He ate the dog food, their children's food, whatever they had to take.

If the farmers had already piled their essentials outside their doors, he ate that too. Never mind what would happen when the 'they' from the radio came and found nothing there. Never mind that.

Johnny ate it all.

Which is why Mr. Clarewater, the small roundish man, had knocked Johnny out with a shovel.

He'd watched Johnny enter into the small vegetable garden behind his farm house. He'd watched Johnny lean over the tomato plants and begin to feast, the red juices mingling on his stained shirt with whatever Johnny had last eaten before wandering into his garden. Mr. Clarewater had watched Johnny become filthy, animal-like – and it gave him hope.

Mr. Clarewater only had tomatoes and a few cans of beans. He was no farmer, but he lived on a farm. He had vast fields for grazing, but behind his house, he had only a small vegetable garden. Not enough to feed them. Not enough to feed him through the winter *and* them. Not nearly enough, in Mr. Clarewater's opinion.

And in Mr. Clarewater's opinion, Johnny was already a victim of circumstance. He was already a roaming animal, and Mr. Clarewater saw nothing wrong in walking up behind him and slamming the back of his steel shovel as hard as he could against the soft spot of Johnny's head.

"They're going to strip this area clean. Eat."

"Mr. Clarewater, I really don't feel good."

"Don't get sick on me. Johnny, if you get sick, you'll never make it. Now, please, eat some more, then you can stop. That'll be enough for today."

Johnny Nishmann had now been eating over at Mr. Clarewater's for a week. Mr. Clarewater had nursed him back to health after beating him with a shovel. It wasn't just the soft spot on the back of his head that Mr. Clarewater had brought his shovel down on, but the shins, ankles, hands, face, and fingers as well. Johnny Nishmann was a mess.

"When will they be here? I thought they were coming soon. Maybe they've come and gone, huh Mr. Clarewater? Can't you get the radio working?"

"Eat one more bite, then rest."

Mr. Clarewater had explained to Johnny several times that when they came and took the little he could offer, what he had piled outside his door, that there would be nothing left to eat the entire winter, so it was important that they ate what they could now. "You see, Johnny, your idiot self actually had the right idea, eating like you had been. But it's not fair for you to eat it all."

Mr. Clarewater told Johnny that he would see to their survival. That Johnny had to be tied. That Mr. Clarewater had to eat, too.

It had to be fair.

This made Johnny cry. He cried not because of the insane man's earlier and terrible brutality or because of the insane man's now terrible kindness, but because the day Mr. Clarewater had attacked him in the garden had not been the first time Johnny had visited Mr. Clarewater's house.

Johnny had eaten his way through neighborhoods and farms, true, but he had done so because he was sneaky.

With the first houses, he'd made a lot of noise, as if it were them outside, taking everything and moving on. But a neighborhood man had peaked and saw that it was just Johnny Nishmann, and Johnny had come under fire. So he got smarter about eating everything he could.

Johnny ditched the neighborhoods and began camping in the woods not far from Mr. Clarewater's farmhouse. He had been hitting up different homes for quite a few days before he had been knocked out with a shovel. And in that time, Johnny had eaten almost every canned good, almost every little packaged, jarred, preserved morsel of food that had been piled nicely in front of those doors.

The sneaky part was that Johnny had carefully, as carefully as a mouse, replaced the cans, filled with dirt, back to where they belonged. He had carefully replaced jars, now filled with moss and water, back in front of doors. He had carefully made it seem as if nothing had been taken. What he took from one home, he used at the next.

So, Johnny cried. He wept because he knew about the switch.

He cried as Mr. Clarewater continued to feed him. He cried as Mr. Clarewater snuck off down to the basement to listen to the dying radio. He cried when Mr. Clarewater said they had only two more days before 'they' came and took everything. Whatever was left, whatever was uneaten, would have to go outside the door with all the cans of food, with all the jars of pickled vegetables, with all the bullets, with everything that Mr. Clarewater had already put out there.

So, Johnny cried. Because Johnny knew what was going to happen when they came to the house. A few vegetables on top of jars of dirt would probably seem like an insult, especially considering how many other houses in the area would have the same thing outside their doors.

All thanks to Johnny.

It might even seem like a little rebellion. Johnny's tears poured down his face, making his food salty. He wondered if they would think the farmers had gotten together and were trying to send a message. What would they think of a message?

Mr. Clarewater knew. They would come inside – unless. Mr. Clarewater knew what they would think if they found jar after jar of moss and water. He knew that if they found tin lids loosely topping cans full of dirt that the 'they' from the radio would come into his house and slit him open like one of the veal cattle he used to raise and butcher before 'they' had starting coming.

They had taken all his steers and cows except two the last time. Mr. Clarewater figured they wanted him to breed them for the next time they came, but he had slaughtered them both over the last year. That was what he knew.

Although he was sure they had left the cattle for him to raise more of, that wasn't something Mr. Clarewater knew. That wasn't how the slaughter business worked. Or, at least, that's not how Mr. Clarewater's veal farm used to operate, to survive.

What he knew, Mr. Clarewater thought to himself as he sharpened his butchering knives in his basement, was that they would be pleased with the salted steaks he'd have out waiting for them, piled high in neat stacks, each individually wrapped in its own brown butcher's paper.

JIM E. WILSON FORGETS YOU

When Jim E. Wilson no longer remembers how to spell the word 'you,' it's time to be careful.

The neighborhood is not the same. Where broken bottles found themselves, now so do fatherless boys, spitting insults from curb to curb. Mothers who yell from ripped screen doors "Be careful out there, it's getting late" have no one to look for across the street. Jim E. Wilson told them so.

"There is no fucking you on this block, on these streets, around the fucking corner," he told one lost and crying maternal unit who was aching to hold her lost and crying little boy. "You is gone. This all belongs to me."

When Jim E. Wilson tells you there is no 'you,' things get simplified. Everything becomes units of measure or pieces of property.

Because when Jim E. Wilson made no difference, just like you, you were a cop and you were my brother.

Jim E. Wilson buys ice cream for the little kids.

"You should see them lick," he tells your partner before getting in the passenger side of the police cruiser. "Let's take a ride with the windows down and talk about whatever it was you wanted us to talk about."

When Jim E. Wilson came to my school, I was a little girl wanting my mother's love and maybe a daddy who didn't dabble in the art of prison tattoos.

You didn't like that, Jim E. Wilson so close to me.

And when Jim E. Wilson walked up the three flights of stairs four years later and pushed open the door to apartment 2B, he stepped over a dead dog and didn't even notice.

It could have been my brother for all he cared. Except you weren't around. You went out one night to do something about Jim E. Wilson and never came home. Sure, we tried to find you, to call you back in, but Jim E. Wilson told us to "Knock it the fuck off. These are my streets. You was disturbing them the other night, looking around, trying to make things a better place, so you is done – forgotten."

We cried a lot that night, Mother and me, and the motherfuckers around the block who always hung around my house. They said, "You ought to do something."

"That's what fucking happened. Get out of my mother's house! Motherfuckers! It ain't like you did anything about it!"

When Jim E. Wilson fills up the gas tank, all the kids watch him and wave. He never pays – except for a little attention to me or any other pretty pretending not to see him stare.

When Jim E. Wilson swallows down the last of the candy, nothing sticks to his teeth. He gets it all in one bite. He always offers the next mouthful to me, then drugs, money, and a whole lot of other sweets to the entire street.

Jim E. Wilson hands it out.

They love him for it. When he walks down the block, they jump up and down yelling "Wait for me!"

When Jim E. Wilson takes them out, he doesn't take them far, and he always lets them in again. When his car stops, they have to go. They always want more or another mile. Whatever they can get, Jim E. Wilson will give. They just have to wait until he drives back around again – "Jump on in, sugar."

The waiting is what kills them, though.

Because when Jim E. Wilson tells them they're out, they're out, standing there next to me on the curb, crying and wishing 'you' were here to do something about it.

Then they remember there is no more you left. Not since Jim E. Wilson had his way.

And when Jim E. Wilson plays polite, my mother always cries to herself and yells at him to get the fuck away from us.

Last Saturday, when Jim E. Wilson closed the door to my mother's room, he mouthed "Look at what you made me do."

So when Jim E. Wilson stood there in apartment 2B two days later, smacking his sugar-coated lips, telling me he "might make you something to remember, sweetie," I stabbed him with a screwdriver four times in the chest, once for each year he'd forgotten, and told him "This is for *you*."

PEANUT BUTTER AND JILLIAN

His lips were warm, not unlike a piece of chocolate left in a child's pocket during a hot afternoon. This struck Jillian as pleasant, her lips against Dylan's warm mushy ones. Jillian kissed them the same way she might push against a pull-only door by accident. When their lips touched, she pulled back, giving Dylan her best you-want-to-play-naughty smile.

Then she thought, *The heck with it.*

She kissed Dylan again.

And again.

Jillian was hungry for lips. For Dylan.

A smile spread across her face, a coy attempt to cover up that hunger. It didn't mean anything, the smile. Not to Jillian.

It did to Dylan.

To him, Jillian's crooked grin equaled danger.

Dylan knew it, that look – someone mad with hunger.

Perhaps this is why Jillian licked her bottom lip seductively.

Or maybe it was because she liked Dylan.

Dylan avoided her smile, resituating himself in an effort to correct the bulge in his brown corduroy pants.

Jillian watched him smooth out his mocha-colored sweater. If he weren't so popular, she'd ask him why he thought wearing an entire outfit the color of cocoa was a good idea.

But he was.

So she didn't.

"This is great," she said, looking deep into Dylan's dark brown eyes.

Dylan nodded apprehensively.

Jillian smiled, licked her top lip, then Dylan's.

This made Dylan nervous. He was afraid of this.

The hunger, his outfit, the kissing – the couch seemed smaller.

Dylan sensed what was in store.

Jillian did not.

It didn't seem special, their making out.

But it was.

For Jillian it meant a lot, not because she liked Dylan or because he loved her, or anything like that at all.

It meant a lot because of her allergies.

Dylan leaned in, kissed her quick, mushy. He wanted it over with, wanted everyone to stop asking why he never made out with girls.

This, Dylan thought, *will shut people up.*

Jillian leaned in, kissed him harder than he'd kissed her, found his bottom lip. Bit hard.

It tasted like peanut butter, maybe chocolate – not what she expected. Dylan's lip, much too soft.

Jillian rolled her tongue across her teeth. *I couldn't have drawn blood*, she thought.

But it didn't taste right.

"Did you eat anything with peanuts in it?"

Dylan smiled and grimaced simultaneously. It was impressive, that smile, awkward and guilty, like a chameleon caught walking over plaid.

Jillian screamed.

Dylan held his bottom lip, pushing peanut butter back inside.

Jillian stared.

Dylan's lip bled peanut butter?

Jillian stared.

Dylan's lip bled *peanut butter.*

Her lip tingled.

Jillian felt it swell, her tongue too.

She tried to breathe, watched creamy tears pour down Dylan's face as he stood, straightening his brown slacks.

She eyed his deep tan skin. She'd always thought he was just Italian.

Her lungs swelled.

If Jillian hadn't been deathly allergic to peanut butter, you could've asked her to describe the rest of the story.

But...

It was like watching the gingerbread man run away.

Dylan stood up, smeared his tears across his cheek, made his way out the same sliding door he'd snuck through earlier.

He stared back at Jillian one more time as he slid the door closed. It was hard for her to see, what with the dying and all, and with the lack of oxygen to her brain, but it looked as if Dylan mouthed something like "I'm just going to tell everyone I'm gay" or "I'm made of peanut butter and chocolate" or "I taste delicious, don't I?" all of which

were probably tricks of the brain.
     Or maybe true.

EVEN TOY SWORDS

When the boy next door knocked on mine and pro-
nounced himself dead, he had a gun and I had a sword.
Because, after all, I was the girl. He said it was only fair,
that I should take what's handed to me. I told him one is as
dangerous as the other and made him promise not to
shoot.

We played until I killed him, one stab through the
heart. His imaginary death was a sight. There was anguish
in his eyes and a sadness in his rolling about my front lawn,
a final peace that belonged only to him, and in the end he
was completely still, stretched out, smiling at what I
couldn't see and what he'd thought must have been the
best neighborly introduction ever.

I never wanted to play such a terrible pretend thing
before, but his performance made me see the merit in a
fight to the death. And I was new to the neighborhood.

Later, when I realized I'd won yet again, that Jon was
dead on my lawn for the third time in one afternoon, I ran

inside yelling hooray. I'm not sure why I was so excited because, as he pointed out, from the very beginning he'd told me that he was the one who was going to die.

When he became a soldier and died in some foreign war, I thought about what I'd done. It was a long time ago, but somehow I still felt responsible.

For me, the wound was fresh. It bled like the time we kissed beneath the stairs at his mother's house, wet and what could have been neverending.

Jon's father lived out of the country, so I was used to him leaving. Every month or so he was gone. It was no different later for us.

In high school, we dated. Sometimes each other.

When we dated other people, Jon told me to stop it with his friends. They had a code and I was breaking it. That seemed silly to me because it was their code, not mine. But he was shocked by what I had done, and I knew right away that he probably loved me.

I told him not to tell me who to date.

He said, "Don't tell me what to do."

We should have argued. Instead we kissed, angry and not knowing what better to do with our lips. He believed in codes and I didn't believe in anything but fake deaths on my front lawn.

When we were married, he told me that college would be around the corner. He thought he'd go into design after he finished the service, but the soldier he was required his will and his body, and I was reluctant to share.

It was a fight to the death he wanted, and I obliged, telling him if he didn't come home soon I'd sell the house and move.

"Where to?" he'd ask.

"Spain," I'd say. It was always somewhere with a beach because those places seemed the most like us – far away and warm to the touch.

"Spain," he'd say. "I hear it's nice there."

I didn't want him to hear me laugh, so I'd cough into the phone and say, "You'll have to hold, I have a young man on the other line."

Whatever he'd say next would always be something that would make me stop crying until he came home.

The next week he'd be back with tickets to the warm country of my choice. He didn't want to go. He couldn't have. He'd just flown in, put his bags on the floor next to our bed, but he'd stand there beside my dresser, helping me fold my clothes. We'd pack and decide what I'd wear when we went dancing.

He'd ask if the new skirt I bought really was vacation material.

"Maybe the beach is cold there now," he'd say. "Maybe we ought to stay in bed."

We played that way and I always won. He was back when I wanted, and he took me where I thought I needed to be.

Our vacations were nice, full of warm sun and full bellies, but he had to leave from time to time.

And I knew somewhere inside of me that one of those times would be the one where I no longer fell asleep on the beach beneath the hot sun knowing someone who loved me would wake me up before I burned.

When he came to my house and I was still only a girl, he would carry all his toys with him, the swords and the guns, but he had other things too. There was a giraffe made out of plastic pieces that he'd assembled in an array of colors. I'd told him "Nothing real looks like what you made with those red, blue, yellow, and green pieces." But, holding out the toy, he asked if I didn't like it anyway. I did, so I had to lie and say it wasn't good enough for me – only a real live animal was a real live animal. Only that would do.

When we were still new at being one person, I told him, "The birds fly just for you, and the snow that fell this morning in our yard landed and piled because you think it's beautiful the day after."

I said to him, "I can't help myself, so I'll help you."

I told him, "We are what you want us to be. We are happy just seeing each other when we can."

I told him those things then.

And I told him those things again, with a choke, sob, and a tear, when they stood me in front of him, laid out for the procession.

I wanted him to know I wasn't playing anymore, not by his code or mine, so I told him, "The toy sword you brought me, I want you to have it back. I'll put it in the casket with Spain, winter snows, and growing old together."

MY SON

My son's second hamster, the blonde teddy bear one, the one he never fed, he's dead and running through my walls.

My son's second hamster, the really furry one, the one who keeps me awake at night, he's hard to see. I can't always get a good look at him, but I know he's there, chewing the wires in my walls.

He eats straight through to all the important parts, spits out the little pieces of rubber and metal debris as if they were no good, as if he were a robot hamster, back from the dead, living only on wire and useless bits of electronics. But only the ones I'm most connected to.

Sometimes I wonder if I'm so different from him. Sometimes I wonder how to count to three.

Those are the times I cry when I'm swinging the hammer to open up my walls. Those are the times I make a mess of drywall and plaster and my wife talks about leaving. She can't remember our trip to Germany, but I can. I can see what she can't, and I can't forget – *eins*, *zwei*, *drei* – I just don't always know what it means.

I can't forget him either. I can't let him run through my house.

Because it's only a matter of time before he finds his way out, and what if there's no wire out there for him to chew?

My son's second hamster has spit out enough of what runs through my walls that I can no longer watch TV or even turn on the lights.

He disappears under my door with the patter of little feet. "Honey, did you see him? He was right there in our doorway."

"No, love, I didn't. Did you? Did you see him again?"

He leads me around the house, but I have a hammer, and now I have holes.

I don't want to miss seeing him, even if it's only in my walls. I can't stand it when I do. Those faint little movements stepping from hole to hole, memory to memory, I don't want to forget them.

Like in Germany, when my little boy jumped into the picture with his mom. He smiled and the wind blew his curly hair across his eyes. I didn't need to see them to know they were blue. He thought he was so cute, shouting the little German he knew.

It was cute enough to put holes in the wall.

My son's second hamster leads me to a different room almost every night, but never Sam's. He won't go in there and neither will my wife. I want to, but not until I catch his dead hamster. Maybe then I'll be able to open his door again.

It's as if the hamster were reliving a memory, running from me like he did when Sam was three and we had returned from our vacation in Europe. But he only escaped once when he was alive, and it makes me wonder whether he really knows where he is or if he's lost somewhere I'll never find him.

My son's second hamster made my wife leave me. She couldn't stand my inability.

He eats real food and talks in German if you catch him. We've only been there once when Sam was three. It's crazy that he remembers Sam or that trip. It's crazy that he remembers Sam knowing a little German, cute as can be.

He didn't even see him there, but he knows Sam stood by the Rhine river, his blonde hair against his big toddler cheeks. He was beautiful and sad and missed his second hamster, the one who keeps me up at night. He missed him like I miss my walls, so much he had to see him.

Now that I've caught him, I've become something of a successful, well-traveled businessman, and I'm getting an official divorce. I sell wire to corporate giants who run it around the world – several times, from what I understand.

My son's second hamster still keeps me up at night, but he's usually in my pocket where I can keep him safe.

He counts off in threes, but I have no idea what he's counting.

I have no idea what I'm counting.

Eins. Zwei. Drei. Ready or not, here I am.

I've replastered the walls and have learned to sleep. On the count of three, I can do almost anything.

I only have to pat my pocket to remember him.

I only have to put my hand there to know how to live, to remember how to do the simplest of things like breathing or eating or remembering what his blonde hair looks like in the wind.

PENNSYLVANIA IS NO CONCERN

Beneath an old sycamore tree, a hiker picked the ground clean of loose sticks.

"What are you doing?"

He looked through the trees, over the branches, at the dirt path he'd come down, searching for who spoke the words, though he knew they came from the sycamore in front of him.

He hesitated. "God?"

"No, I am a tree."

"You must get that a lot then."

"No, I am a tree."

"Yeah, that's the thing."

"What?"

"You're a *tree*."

"Yes."

"I'm a person. You're a tree. I pick up your fallen branches and you are still a tree."

"Why?"

"Why am I a person and you a tree? Or why am I picking up your branches?"

"The branches."

"I'm going to burn them."

"Burn? For fire?"

"Does that bother you?"

"They are the dead of me. Take them."

"Thanks."

"I have never seen fire, though. Will you burn close to me?"

"I guess. I mean, yeah, I'll burn *them*. I don't know. I feel like I shouldn't. It seems dangerous or perverse or something."

"Please."

The hiker dug a small pit in the earth and placed the branches he'd gathered into the hole until he'd formed a teepee-like construction.

The tree watched, concerned by the method, but said nothing as trees are prone to do.

The hiker shoved pine needles, a cotton ball, and tiny baby twigs, the thin dead that litter the forest floor, into the center of the teepee of broken branches.

The tree asked the hiker if that was fire.

Staring at the pit, at the wood in teepee form, a strange monument of sticks pointing to the sky, the hiker was struck by a thought – he had made his own tree, an odd version of one at least, and it seemed significant and the hiker thought of not setting fire to it, of lying to the sycamore. *Maybe*, the hiker thought, *the tree would be better thinking man warmed himself next to a wooden shrine, a rough semblance of a living tree.* It was real enough, he considered, and if the tree thought this was fire, an odd version of itself made from fallen branches, then he ought to let it.

The tree asked again about whether or not this is what hikers call fire and if the branches were now considered burning.

When the hiker did not answer, the tree wanted to know if he would sleep next to the pit where the branches were built into a teepee and if that made the hiker feel warm and comforted to lie so close.

The hiker hesitated.

The sycamore continued, asking the difference between warm and cold and whether there was one between hot and comfort.

The hiker did not answer, but took out his flint and steel and told the tree he had not finished the fire.

Striking steel against flint, the hiker threw crackling sparks onto the pine needles and cotton ball and little baby twigs that had once blanketed the forest floor.

When the cotton caught, when the pine needles smoldered, and when the little baby twigs cracked and flamed, the tree watched, concerned by the rapid consumption.

The sycamore was used to a gradual disappearance, its branches dissolving into the earth, becoming part of the soil that nourished him.

The fire was fast and the tree watched life and death and all that occurred in between, as far as it was concerned.

After the fire took to a steady burn, the hiker sat down and waited for the sycamore to speak.

There was silence and he was afraid the tree had seen too much or he had made this up and that this was what he was afraid of, the reason he started the hike – a separation from reality.

He began to talk to the tree.

"The Horse-Shoe Trail is barren of people," he told the sycamore, "a nice parting of ways from the Appalachian where hikers travel for pictures, shit trophies of *I've done it* to ooh and ahh at."

"What do they take pictures of?"

"You. Trees. Sometimes mountainsides."

"They take pictures of me? Of trees? Why?"

"They think you're beautiful. I do too."

"What?"

"I don't mean you personally. I mean trees in general. People appreciate them."

"You burn us in fires."

"For warmth and light. It's another reason we love you."

"You love me?"

"No. I guess not really."

"I love the fire."

"Do you? Why?"

"It's fast and alive."

"I guess. Would you talk to another hiker if one came by? I need to know this is real."

"What is real?"

"This — us talking."

"Why don't you burn yourself? Fire is real. I know that now."

"What? No. I mean, yes, but no. I'm not going to set myself on fire. I know I'm real. I know the fire is real. I don't know if you talking to me is."

By the fire the hiker waited for what was real and the comfortable flames warmed him and the rhythm of sleep found him and the large sycamore began to bend.

The tree did so slowly and there were cracks and breaks that came with the stiffness and the bending and they were loud but did not wake the hiker who dreamed of his work in a high school where his building administrator observed the children who did not respect him and they laughed at the hiker in his dream and the administrator noted it, penning down his failure to engage the children in the subject he loved most.

I know what is real, the sycamore thought, and the tree bent hard at the trunk, pushing its branches closer to the man and the fire.

I am real, the sycamore considered, dipping its boughs into the white embers and orange flames.

The tree burned and the hiker dreamed and when he woke the forest was bright in the night with hot flames and the hiker listened to the sycamore moan and to the fire's draw of air, a rapid consumption of life that sounded real like a burning tree in pain or like a hiker crying through a panic attack beneath the Pennsylvania stars.

A LITERARY GOD (IN LOVE)

I was the classic angsty narrator, pessimistic, brooding, searching for something until I found it. I stopped here, there, learned lessons, developed into something greater, but I was no symbol. So I took a puff of my cigarette, leaned against the brick wall of the university, and thought, *Only one other person in this world understands me.*

Just one.

Her.

I exhaled, waited for something to happen, knew it wouldn't, and went into the library.

It's where Sara goes after class.

And if anyone understands me, it's her. At least she will, I know, by Chapter 43. She's written just for me, I can tell, so when I find her sitting in the very back, scrunched up in a *Harry Potter* novel, I tap her book gently.

"Sara," I say, "you're the girl I'm supposed to meet. Right here. I know it. Give me a chance?"

She laughs, turns a page.

"I promise I'll make you happy. You won't regret it," I say. "We'll go to dinner, discover we like the same music."

She flips again.

"We'll eat at this little corner place – it used to be a book shop. I'll order what you want, you'll order what I want, we'll switch after the first mouthful. It'll be perfect, just wait."

Sara turns the page, doesn't look up, and even worse – I can't remember if it's a *Harry Potter* book or some other one. I know in my book she's reading, but what if it's not this one?

What if we're only in Chapter 42?

"Sara," I say, "can I tell you something?"

Her page turns. She's heard this before. I've told her at least three times since I cut Modern Lit and spent the night in the library, since I found her in the morning, sitting in the back corner, just like I'd read she'd be.

"Sara, this is real," I say. "I know you. I knew your name before I made it down the library stairs, before I said hello. I understand what's going on. I do."

She yawns, turns a page.

"Sara. You, me – we're going to make willow trees weep. We're going to love each other the way that only happens in stories. I get it – who I am, what I'm looking for, where I'm going. It's you."

Sara starts to close the book, stops.

"Wait 'til I tell you about Chapter 44. Oh my God, Chapter 44. You're gonna cry, maybe hug me. I can't wait. I can't."

But Sara, she doesn't believe me. Not at all. I can tell because she goes back to reading the same chapter of *Harry Potter* she started on before I interrupted.

But that's the thing – Sara rereading the chapter, me

interrupting – it's just like in the book. It has to be her.

"Hey," I say, "what if I prove it? What if I find that book I told you about?"

Sara looks up, smiles, and it's better than the ending of any story. She's so pretty, and she gets me. She understands more than she knows.

"Oh yeah," she says, "the book about us? The one you found in here but can't ever seem to locate?"

"Yeah, that's the one," I say, keeping my eyes on her hazelnut hair, all curls like it's described in chapter one. Her eyes roll and it drives me bananas. God, she's the cutest thing. Not just because in my book she loves me and we get married. No, because she really is – beautiful.

There it is on the shelf – a book about me. I flip through and it's all there. Everything up 'til the moment I reach for it. Better yet, the part where Sara takes it from my nervous hands, puts down *Harry Potter*, and reads – it's there. Her turning page after page of our world. It's magic. We're magic.

At least I think it reads that way. To me anyway.

It's so perfect with her. Chapter 12, when she sprains her ankle, I tell her it's okay because I own a magic carpet, then swing her onto my back. We zoom down the street, away from the bar, pretending we're flying the whole time, all the way back to our apartment where I kiss her because she has these little tears in her eyes and I can tell it still hurts.

Every page with her is a better story.

And it's real. I mean, I knew it was. That this book was about us. That I'd find it again. That what I'd read was about me, about Sara. It's just I wasn't sure because I skipped a few chapters the first time. In fact, I really didn't pay attention or get close to figuring out the book was about me until the page where I met Sara.

The stuff before didn't even make sense.

Didn't matter.

Because after Sara, my narration seems so on point, like I really get how this story works, how I should tell it. It's like I understand what's important – the rising action, how it should climax. All of it.

And it's there. In my book. The pages explain it.

I'm a first-person omniscient narrator because reading my story, reading it aloud to myself, it's like having God whisper the answers to all my questions, but better because I'm the one doing it. They're my answers.

Me telling it.

And I understand exactly what's going on, like why I kiss Sara in the back of the library even though she hasn't finished reading Chapter 15.

In the book, I take it slowly out of her hand, brush her hair out of the way, and meet her eyes with mine. When we look at each other, she knows how much I love her. She's just read it. She says, "Excuse me, your book? It's *our* story. It's *our* book." She says it just like that and we kiss. We both cry big tears that drip salt all over our lips because that's what happens – eighth paragraph, page 200, Chapter 43.

That's how I describe it.

Because I love the way we read. I love our story.

HER HEART A THUNDERING STEED

Sara's little heart baffled the doctor.

It sounded different to different people.

Sara's doctor heard drums.

Boom.

Bang.

Boom.

"Hey, nurse," he said. "Do you hear tom-toms?"

The nurse lowered her ear to Sara's baby soft chest, and there it was – a humming frog singing solo beneath the Pennsylvania stars.

"No," she said.

"Are you sure?" asked the doctor.

"Yes," said the nurse, her ear against Sara. "It's beautiful. It sounds like a child full of love."

She lied.

It sounded like frogs and a river crashing against granite, like Yellowstone wolves running through ravines and howling echoes.

Doctor Bom said, "Yes, indeed, I hear a girl who's going to be just wonderful."

He felt awkward

and lied, too.

They couldn't tell Sara's mother her daughter's heart sounded like Glacier National Park, like you wouldn't know unless you've been there, like bubbles popping, soap sudding on a messy baby face.

They couldn't tell her that any more than you could.

No

way

at

all.

Boom.

Bam.

Boom.

Mother cradled baby,

baby cradled breast, the heartbeat running water over million-year-old pebbles, smooth pops, low ripples.

Sara's mother listened.

It reminded her of a man,

of a piece of elevator music,

of a song she fell in love with.

She stood there next to him, bobbing her head to the rhythm, traveling up, up, up.

He wore a white coat and hummed along to the violins and cellos.

He was not her husband,

but she loved him,

like an unspoken connection,

like his eyes – green, soft grass.

Sara's mother stood with him.

Monday.

Tuesday.

Wednesday and Thursday.

On Fridays he worked from home, he said.

"Oh," she said, "must be nice."

It was.

But they loved each other and neither told the other and that wasn't.

That wasn't nice at all.

And it hurt her mother's heart to hear Sara's own tiny organ sound so much like jazz played through an elevator speaker.

Because it sounded like him,

like love for no reason,

like not expressing how your heart feels.

Sara's heart, a favorite song played on repeat.

Sara's heart, a man in an elevator tapping his foot.

Sara's heart, her mother loves him.

Sara's heart, his name was Sam.

Unlike Doctor Bom, Sam was a cardiologist.

He worked on the 34th floor for thirteen years.

He examined chest x-rays and loved Nirvana.

The band, not the heavenly place.

Hell wasn't nearly as loud.

Sara's mother knew that. She wore sadness like a wool knit hat.

It covered her ears.

But baby Sara's heart blew bass drum bumps through sad.

No matter what.

It was that loud.

Boom.

Bang.

Bam.

Boom.

"Sounds steady," said Sara's father, "like traffic in the rain."

He wiped his forehead, the one Sara's mother never fell in love with, and he stared out the hospital window down at the street below.

He didn't know about the cardiologist or the elevator rides,

but he had a feeling.

The feeling was a car driving away, his wife inside, traveling down a quiet street and not looking back.

He stared at the rain falling. It soaked the street below.

He worked there, on the street. His badge and gun said so.

His policeman's mare neighed and said so, too.

The beast trod iron on broken asphalt roads and galloped after criminals.

Sara's heart was loud like a horse, too.

Not a pink pony floating on a cloud,

like a thundering steed.

It was excited by life.

It was young

and strong

and fast

and ready.

Her father's gun had six bullets in it and sounded like a glass bottle broken in Hell.

Sara's mother heard it once.

It had been an accident.

Sara wasn't.

There's no such thing as that.

Because.

Sara's heart pounded away and when her father leaned over her and smiled, Sara's heart sounded like June waves on white shores, like motocross in Alabama.

"She's happy, I think," said Sara's father.

"Maybe," said Sara's mother.

Sara's father could hear the difference.

But he couldn't hear his wife's heart at all.

Not when he smiled at her.

He knew that.

He knew some love was different. Some love sounded like his daughter and some love didn't sound at all, even if you wanted it to play the brass section at your fifth grade recital, even if you wanted it to drop the bass or shout its feelings for you so strong that kids at clubs would dance dirty to it.

Some love was Sara's mother.

Sara's father was okay with that.

It hurt, but he loved motocross and Ocean City, New Jersey.

So not too bad, a daughter's heart pounding like Alabama and salt water waves.

So not too bad, your wife loves another man.

So not too bad, he loves her back, serenaded in elevator music.

So not too bad, as long as you hear it – Sara's heart, the traffic of love, in the small of the hospital room far above the city streets.

The Boom
  Bang
  Boom
  continued. And Sara grew. Louder. Different. In other ways.

In the fifth grade, Thomas Fields transferred schools.

He came from Ohio.

The teacher said, "Thomas, you can sit next to Sara."

Thomas stood there, straw straight in a field of desks.

He couldn't hear Mrs. Benson,

only birds belting a tune like Heaven is snowing and the angels have the day off.

Sara turned robin-belly red.

"Is that you?" Thomas asked.

He had to shout.

"IS THAT YOU?"

Sara shook her head yes.

"Cool."

But it wasn't always.

"Sometimes your heart betrays you," Sara's mother said.

And it did.

When Sara hugged her father goodbye, it sounded like a fast red car zipping down the expressway.

And when Sara's mother stood in her doorway, checking to see if she'd finished her homework, it sounded like fake snoring and 'Go away, my headphones are in' and 'I know you won't come in, Mom. That would mean you'd have to talk to me.'

It told the truth, Sara's heart.

One way

or another.

When Sara stood next to Thomas, her heart sounded like your elementary school talent show. The loud one where Arnold Sheperdson played his dad's accordion.

And when Sara's mother left the kitchen, her father at the table, eyes wet from some awful truth, Sara's heart sounded like 'Why can't you two ever be in the same room together?' It sounded like that and a bunch of angry tears, like thirteen on fire, like 'Mommy, you need to love Daddy,' like 'Dad, why can't you be home more?'

Sara's heart was 'You can't just love me. C'mon, guys.'

Boom.

Bam.

Boom.

Sara stood at the front door.

"I'm going to Thomas's house," she said.

"What?" her mother yelled.

"I'M GOING TO THOMAS'S HOUSE!"

Kaboom.

Time with Thomas was Sara's heart whacked out on street drugs.

It was Woodstock so loud.

It was free love.

Totally high.

So high.

High on Thomas time.

Sara's heart beat Thomas, best friend since fifth grade, and pounded out encores.

It was hundreds of Saras chanting his name.

Sara and Thomas, inseparable hippy gods.

Sara kissed her mother goodbye on the cheek.

Her mother said, "I love you. Be safe."

Sara looked away, her heart crickets chirping.

She didn't believe her mother,

that she was capable of real emotion.

Sara didn't know about Sam the cardiologist

or the elevator rides

or the music that may have come from an elevator speaker

or from a heart similar to her own.
Sara thought her mother was messed up or something.
She was kind of right.
Sara's mother was sort of broken,
confused and fragmented from loving someone else,
so she tried to be careful all the time,
no matter who she was around.
Sara's mother was afraid her heart would betray her, thumping off some out of tune melody no one would recognize.

Sara closed the door
    and left for Thomas's.
    Her mother smiled small and sad on the other side. She wanted a cherry red sportster revving its hot-to-trot engine. She wanted
    Boom
    Bang
    Boom
    on overdrive,
    but Sara's heart, an empty field, occasional cricket, betrayed her.
    It never learned to hide
    how it felt
    about
    anyone.
    Not like her mother.

Once, when Sara was only thirteen, she ran away, and her parents found her by flashlights and listening.
    She was so sad,
    like 'Help me, it hurts' sad,
    turtle in love with bird sad,

like Portuguese man o' war in love with a fisherman's net sad,

and 'I just want this to stop, this isn't fair, why him, God?' sad.

She was that sad,

and her parents heard her – a dripping faucet.

Plop.

Plop.

Plop.

Sara's heart betrayed her, and her father the policeman and her mother the star-crossed lover gently opened the clubhouse door.

The clubhouse was down the street and belonged to their neighbor, Thomas.

At one point he was new to the neighborhood, but now he felt old and young at the same time.

Sara swaddled him in her arms.

Thomas told her parents, "Ah, you can't be here. This is private property. You should leave."

"Thomas," they said, "we love you."

They kissed his forehead.

It felt hot,

and it began to rain, or maybe everyone was crying.

Sara's parents scooped her up and carried her down out of the elm tree fort.

Left inside the clubhouse was Thomas and his cancer.

It was bad.

"Thomas is no reason to try," Sara said into the night, "but you have to anyway."

"Thomas is exactly that," whispered Sara's mother, but no one heard her. She'd walked ahead, keeping some distance.

In Thomas's hospital room, after the doctor said the words "some progress," there was a marching band and a seven-gun salute and a hot air balloon filling with flame, and all of that, so much of that.

Sara's doing.

Thomas slept.

Sara hid in her father's shoulder and he wrapped her in his arms and it seemed like he could cry.

But he didn't.

He listened instead and waited for Sara to sound herself to sleep, her heart beating *Apocalypse Now*, her heart beating a prelude to your last winter in Greece.

It came as he knew it would and Sara's father listened to the waves against the shore, the steady rhythm of traffic he heard when Sara slept, her head nuzzled against his chest, close to his heart.

He cried that night,

her head against him.

The occasional sound of Sara's heart breaking,

of wildfires,

of landmines,

of fault lines,

of fathers holding daughters who will never be the same.

He held her and felt an earthquake.

The earthquake was him.

He cried and shook

and cried and shook

until Sara's mother came into the room.

Without a sound, she leaned down and kissed his forehead and swept back his gray hair, but no matter how she tried, he shook.

Until it was over.

"She hurts so badly," he said to Sara's mother.

"It'll quiet down."

"Can you really control that thing?" Sara's father asked.

He put his hand on Sara's mother's

and squeezed.

"Thomas makes you think of things," he said.

"No," she said.

"Of how little time we have to be honest with ourselves," he said.

Sara's mother looked away, her thoughts on elevators and sweet jazz, on standing in doorways and doors shut tight.

Sara's mother lied,

like doctors and nurses,

like fathers and mothers,

like husbands and wives,

like daughters with their hearts broken.

"Stop it. You're talking nonsense," Sara's mother said.

Sara's father stared at the puddle on the linoleum. It came from the feet standing behind him. Sara's mother shook.

Nirvana's "All Apologies" played in the background.

It was faint, like batteries giving up.

"Stop," Sara's mother said.

The puddle grew.

 Beneath the chair, feet swam.

"Stop what?" he asked.

Sara's mother put a hand to her chest.

Sara, sixteen with a license,

Boom

Bang

Boom,

was asked not to drive by her own father.

He was afraid.

"When you get angry at other drivers, it sounds like you're blaring the horn."

Sara said, "I am, Dad."

"Oh, well, you shouldn't."

"Is that it?" Sara asked.

"No, there've been complaints that your heart sounds like an F1 race car."

"Dad!"

"You scared Miss Winlin."

Boom.

Bam.

Boom.

"I'm going to pick up Thomas and take him to his treatment," Sara said.

"Okay, well, be safe and tell Thomas no funny business in the car or I'll arrest him."

Sara shot a look, her heartbeat 'Oh my God, Dad, really?'

"Love you."

"I know," Sara said.

When Sara was eighteen, an acceptance letter came in the mail.

She held it in her hand. She read the contents again. It was true. Her heart was going to college.

It pumped an extra beat.

Boom.

From upstairs, Sara's super mature heart sounded like

'Mom, I don't have to deal with you,' like 'Dad, you can't watch me now,' like humming and packing, like laughing and beers cracking, like 'I'm older now.'

Sara raced around the house, letter in hand. A flag.

Victory.

Freedom.

"Careful! You'll hurt yourself," said Sara's mother. She stood in the kitchen doorway.

Sara's heart a balloon deflating.

"You scared me," Sara said.

"Sorry, I didn't mean to."

"You never mean anything."

Sara left the room.

Silence. Not a beat.

No boom.

No bang.

Sara's mother followed her upstairs.

The steps were nothing like an elevator.

No pleasing music.

No Sam the cardiologist loving her back through the eyes,

no steady line of care,

thoughtful questions,

kind concern.

Nothing like that at all.

"I love you and I'm happy for you. St. John's University is what you wanted. I just want you to promise me something," Sara's mother said.

Sara sat on her bed.

Her bed was shaped like a police car. A fast one. It was a twin Sara could have traded in for a full.

She didn't.

Sometimes at night Sara would lie in her police car.

In her room, it sounded like the rain.

It came from her chest,

a steady downpour

of Thomas,

of 'I love you,'

of 'Will you be okay?'

Sara sat on the edge of her bed, staring at her mother in the doorway.

"You love me?" asked Sara.

"Yes, and I want you to promise me something."

"Do you love Dad?"

"I want you to try and date other people."

Boom.

Bang.

Boom.

"Dad, do you think Mom is happy?"

Sara's father sat down

and told her of first dates, of sleigh bells ringing, of smooth jazz fuzz from lo-fi heart speakers.

He told her of fading, of soundproofing and dampers, of silence and waiting, of suspicions and doctors.

Sara cried.

Her father sniffled.

"I know this a fucked up thing to say, but I can understand why she might be that way. You're never home. But why is she like that with me?"

Sara's father, the silent type, the policeman who owned a gun type, the gun that sounded like Hell through a broken window type, stood up and put his hand on Sara's shoulder.

"She loves you as much as I do."

"Then what is it?"

"I think it's broken."

"I'm going to Thomas's."

BOOM.

Sara stood next to Thomas,

and held his hand.

He smiled.

Sara's heart pounded hot summer nights on the boardwalk,

like July fireworks

over the ocean.

Thomas had an appointment.

It was in the same building where Sara's mother worked.

"If we see your mom here," Thomas said, "it might be a good time to tell her."

Sara agreed, her heart playing an awesome rock song, the chorus 'Thomas and Sara go to college, though he never applied.'

Thomas is a year off to make art, twisting wire and clay.

Thomas is a sculpture,

a bluebird inside an old man's chest,

perched on a little swing,

that Sara loves.

"Hi, Thomas. Sara, what are you doing here?"

Inside the elevator, jazz played.

"Thomas is coming with me."

Sara leaned against the elevator wall, her head against the speaker.

It was broken.

A repairman had received complaints.

There was nothing he could do.

Not within budget.

Sara moved her head away from the speaker.

There it was.

Elevator music,

lo-fi treble and fuzz bass.

"Mom?"

Sara's mother stood awkwardly rubbing her shoes together, her head bent down.

Next to her, a cardiologist smiled.

Only inches separated them.

Sara watched the doctor's green eyes fall onto her mother.

They were soft,

like covering her with a blanket and sipping chicken soup,

like twenty-five years of wanting to say 'I love you.'

Sara listened to the elevator music

her mother played.

It was a slow build,

like a mother and daughter finding common ground,

like Sara's heart, a new rhythm of understanding.

BEER OF THE MONTH

"Sam, you have to get out, be part of something. I know it's hard, but they're gone. Sitting here alone, it's no good. You need to meet people – a girl, even."

My Poppy, he cares a lot about me. It shows.

He rubs my back in small circles, says, "Why not try a beer of the month club. It'll be a nice start, a step, you know? You like to write. You like to drink. You could drink different beers, write about them. They have a newsletter. It'll be nice."

"Sure, Poppy. That sounds good."

And it is.

The first beer, a stout, is delicious – not terrible, not bitter. The second, a blond from France, pours with too big a head. It makes me thirsty, much too sweet. The porter, though, it's nothing special, like me – and I love it. The beer of the month club sends a newsletter with their variety pack, and in the letter an offer for any member to contribute, to write in, to meet them (if you're local) at a pub in the city, so I write:

> *Dear Beer of the Month Club Friends,*
>
> *Let's talk — Broken Bottle's Vanilla Porter!*
>
> *Unlike the Devil's HopImp, which supports a bitter finish hinting of marijuana, Broken Bottle's Porter suggests a mild fall day dipped in chocolate. Not ironically, the vanilla takes a backseat to the warm coffee and dark chocolate aromas highlighted in the first taste of this beer. However, it's Broken Bottle's smooth aftertaste that is so everyday, so vanilla, so ordinary and painless — so Monday through Wednesday.*
>
> *It's vanilla through and through.*
>
> *Like, for instance, say you were drinking the porter, like I was, on a porch overlooking your neighbor's front yard. You could enjoy its smoothness so quietly that when your married neighbors arrive home, happy and in love, they wouldn't even notice you, not even as you stand there with your pint glass in hand, watching them kiss, lowering their hands to each other's soft spots. They'd go at it for the entire brew. Why? Because it's vanilla, non-interrupting, harmless, alone, waiting to be paired, the complement to something bigger than itself.*
>
> *Drink it alone or from afar in the company of others.*
>
> *Sincerely,*
>
> *Sam R. Rulik*

When next month's variety pack comes, I tear through the packaging to see if my piece on the porter is in the newsletter. It's not a big deal if they don't put it in – but they do. There it is, right next to some schlub's thoughts on the New Water Stout.

I'm part of something.

And on the newsletter, on the back, offers for other clubs. A chocolate of the month, a flower of the month, a song of the month – so many more things to enjoy, to make my life full. Poppy's right – it's nice. I can feel myself slowly working out of the funk I've been in since I lost them. Sure I'm not exactly out there falling in love yet or finding someone to restore my faith in humanity, but chocolate sounds good to me, and for $65 they send you two varieties from two different chocolatiers each month, and the best part is they have a newsletter you can write in to. Members only.

Dear Chocolate of the Month Club Family,

Let's discuss the coy devilishness of Wisconsin native and chocolatier Daryl Wyettson's Maple-Infused Dark Chocolate!

When I eat chocolate, I like to have my mouth whisked away to a romantic dinner in Europe, but the Maple-Infused Dark Chocolate, although interesting, leaves you and your taste buds alone in the woods, which might be where you were eating anyway if you're like me and you don't have a dog or a girl or really anyone at all besides your grandfather to share your chocolate with. But I wouldn't really call it sharing when Poppy comes and tries to take it all. That's why you, if you're like me, have to hightail it out to the woods behind your house and eat it alone there, chocolate by chocolate.

And when you bite into Daryl Wyettson's Maple-Infused Dark Chocolate, you feel like crying, not because you have to eat it by yourself surrounded by a few pine trees far out in your yard, or because you're afraid Poppy will think you're rude for not sharing, but because you're part of something. If you're like me, when you bite into that dark chocolate and it tastes like delicious bitter sweetness followed by mellow Sunday morning breakfast syrup, you cry because it reminds you of just that – breakfast with mom and dad, how your father would hold your mother, wrapping his arms around her while she made the pancakes. It reminds you, if you're like me, of them, of you and them together.

Wyettson's Maple-Infused Dark Chocolate – chocolate that makes you cry. Take that for what it's worth.

Sincerely,
Sam R. Rulik

My grandfather reads my little column in the Chocolate of the Month Club newsletter. "It's good, Sam. Weird, but good. Why don't you go out, maybe meet some of the club members? Maybe you could even bring your two clubs together, huh?"

"I don't know, Poppy," I say, "the beer club is pretty exclusive. I wouldn't want to ruffle any feathers. Besides, did you see the back of the Chocolate of the Month newsletter? There are other clubs advertised there, ones I didn't know existed. And they've got newsletters, too."

"That's good, Sam. Maybe you could meet some of their members."

"Yeah, maybe."

My grandfather, Poppy, I can tell, he's not so sure about me writing to these clubs. I tell him, "Poppy, I paid my dues. I'm part of them," and he puts down the most recent newsletter for the Bird of the Month club. My canary, September's bird, she sits on her perch. She watches, bounces nervously. But that's the nature of canaries, or so I've learned. Poppy, though, he's not usually this nervous. It's not like him. He wants to say something, but he's afraid to, concerned he'll scare me off and I'll stop trying again. That I'll be alone, a tribe of one. That other people will hurt me.

"What's great," I say to Poppy while looking straight into his eyes, the same steel blue eyes my father had, "is everyone who reads the newsletter is a club member, Poppy. You know, someone with the same interests – same likes and dislikes as me."

He looks troubled, shifts his weight, uncomfortable.

"These readers, they're potential friends. Maybe more than that one day. Who knows? There might be someone in one of these clubs who, I don't know, might be my future *best* friend, maybe. You know, like Dad was to Mom and vice versa. They were best friends, not just husband and wife, right? You could tell with them, couldn't you, Poppy?"

My grandfather, he sits down, takes a deep breath, the kind he takes when he says his heart hurts.

I know the feeling.

Dear Bird of the Month Club Friends,

Of all the birds we've had flown to our homes these past few months, let's be honest – none compare to the Australian Love Birds. Corny, yes (everyone loves a pair of love birds, right?), but beautiful and soft-twilled as well. Their eyes lock on their soulmate (kindly included in July's shipment – two for the price of one!) and just about never leave. What's so nice about these birds is nothing else matters to them. You? It doesn't matter about you. They're not concerned. If you're like me, you figured this out, watching those love birds ignore the world around them, even as it came crashing down.

For me, it was quite literally when my grandfather, whom I live with, knocked over their cage while vacuuming. I screamed, "Poppy! Look what you've done! My birds, they'll die from shock." And my Poppy, well, he couldn't hear a lick above the noise of the vacuum sweeping the rug, sucking up all those extra seeds. That's when I noticed, despite my shouting loud enough to be heard over the vacuum, despite the thunder of that machine in my grandfather's hands, despite the fact that their very home dropped off the cliff of my counter, the Australian Love Birds, coupled for life, stared at each other. They never wavered, never drifted apart during any of the danger. None of it mattered to them as long as they had each other.

If you're like me, you'll find the Australian Love Birds by far the most soothing, peaceful pet birds you'll add to your collection. They're like having model parents right there for you, showing you how to love, how to lean on the other, how to ignore the small stuff. They're the perfect couple to show you how it's done, especially when there's no one else there to show you.

Much Love,
Sam R. Rulik

Dog of the Month. Kitten of the Month. Friend of the Month. Color of the Month. Bacon of the Month. Fish of the Month. Ethnicity of the Month. Canned Food of the Month. Language of the Month.

There are so many.

I'm torn between Indian of the Month or Native American of the Month. Americanized take-out or warring discontent and forced drinking. I decide on Tribe of the Month and start with Lenape. For an entire month I gather berries, clear paths, pull thin strips of bark from trees, make string for a longhouse I never want to sleep in – but sleep I do until the month is over.

The month of September – Mohawk. And I think about killing my neighbor. Poppy says "This club needs to relax." And I drink firewater only to wake up another month later not part of anything, wondering if the next club might have a newsletter, something more loving than a tribe of people saying "Kill the buffalo, Sam. Kill for the people."

A tribe is a family. A family a tribe. A club a month. A month a family. A people full of family.

Poppy slams the door, storms into the kitchen. "Kid of the month! This has gone too far, Sam. God, they can't be serious, sending you a different child each month. That's insanity. There are documents, shots, medicine needed for children."

Poppy's on edge, has been since he found out about my new club. He won't sit down to look at the picture of the November kid, a cute one with red curly hair.

"Poppy, don't be crazy. You don't keep 'em. They're kids. You return them at the end of the month. All you do is pin the *unaccompanied minor* tags, which are included, to their backs, and – BAM – you're good to go."

My grandfather sits down, folds his hands. "You know, your parents loved you so much that they wanted more kids. Did you know that?"

He's never mentioned this detail before, my parents wanting to supply me with brothers and sisters, wanting to keep the baby train chugging along. Not that it matters. It's not like they had the chance. So I say to him, "Yeah, that's nice, Poppy. I think after a few months of this club, I'll feel the same way." Then I give him a warm smile. Grandfathers live for warm smiles.

Then we stare across the kitchen at each other.

Then we both smile.

Poppy watches me, takes in how calm I am at the mention of my parents. He's looking for something: hurt in the eyes, a flash of pain I haven't yet rid myself of.

But he doesn't see it.

So we smile some more.

Because I'm getting better. "It's these clubs," I say before he can talk. "I'm figuring it out, whatever it is."

He goes in for a hug, then stops. "But this club, this is absurd, Sam. Send the kid back."

"Shh," I tell him, "October is upstairs. He'll hear you."

"Christ, does he even have a name?"

He does, and I tell Poppy October's kid is Simon, a twelve-year-old who I'm not a huge fan of. He's already kicked me in the shin, eaten the ice cream, and hugged me way too much.

"What gives with kids?" I ask Poppy. "One moment Simon hates his room, the next he wants to watch a movie on the couch with me."

Poppy shrugs, puts a hand on my shoulders, says, "It's a learning, loving experience."

Simon doesn't make any sense at all, but man, can he run. I mean, I started jogging after the Shoe of the Month Club sent me a great minimalist trailrunner for the month of September, and it's really nice to get out there and all. I even see the same runners day in and day out, but we don't really run together – not yet. But, Simon, he runs with me, even if he's sure as Hell confusing, but maybe that's how kids are. They're weird at heart, that's all. And Hell, it's nice to have someone right there beside me, keeping pace, even if sometimes I think he's just trying to kick me in the back of the foot or beat me in some imaginary race. It's still nice.

Dear Kid of the Month Club Loved Ones,

Oh man, how much did you love Theodore? But please! Never send me a three-year-old again!

And Simon! What a kid! Man, can he move! What an athlete! Sure makes any parent proud – but watch out, right? There's an angry streak in that one.

And then, club members, my loved ones, there's little Meadow June. Oh, man, she broke my heart. In fact, I've decided to keep her, to be her father. I'm sorry to all those future club members, but I just can't send her back – she won't let me! She's the bossiest little one-and-a-half-year-old I've ever met. And Poppy, my grandfather, he won't admit it, but just the thought of her leaving makes him tear up. In fact, he's the one who hinted at the idea of dipping into the inheritance and paying that ASTRONOMICAL fee the club charges if you want to keep.

But I know you understand, because if you're like me, and you had little Meadow June with you, you sat her on the counter while you cooked, and she just watched you and smiled. You couldn't even walk past her, not if you're like me, because she'd say "Dada" and reach out those two little pudgy arms of hers for you to lift her up by. And really, she just wants you to hold her, to lay her head on your chest. She's your biggest fan and you didn't even do anything – she can't even read your awesome newsletter columns – she just loves you and wants you to be with her all the time, and that's something. Alright, maybe you do everything for her she could possibly ever need you to, but she loves you for you. And those blue eyes, those little blonde curls, the way she walks with her belly pushed out like a little slugger.

That's all I have to say about that one!
Thanks and sorry, club members!
With unconditional love,
Sam R. Rulik

After Kid of the Month Club, Girl of the Month Club doesn't seem like a big deal, not at all, not until Beth hits me. She's drunk and totally resents me for being able to work from home. I try telling her that between my inheritance, the civil suit Poppy won for my grief, and the freelance editing I do that we have plenty, that little Meadow June is well cared for, that there's no real pressure for her to go out and work a job she doesn't love. But Beth – wow. She drinks down her shitty beer, hits me in the arm, whips her well-manicured hand out so her fingers snake bite a soft spot, and there's that explosion of pain. Sharp. Then she acts like she's kidding, teasing me, not that angry at all. But even Poppy's afraid and Meadow June gets scared, reaches for me. When she does, that makes Beth angrier, like Meadow loves only me or something, but that's not it, I try telling her. I say, "She's just scared when you're loud." But Beth – boy, can she scream. And it makes me hate January. Hate it.

February. That's a different story. It's so different I write in about it because it's so good, so what everything should always be forever and ever. It's so good it makes me understand everything a little better – my parents's funeral, Meadow June, Poppy, every club, every day of the week, month, year.

Really, it does.

She makes everything better.

Dear Girl of the Month Club Frenemies,

No hard feelings, but I'm keeping Sara. I know, I know, that's not fair, not everyone has the equivalent of a down payment on an obnoxiously large house in the suburbs, but it's not just me. It's her. Sara. She loves me, too. So much so, she's paying everything she has to be with me. Sure, things will be a bit tight, but it's worth it. Because, if you're like me, when Sara is around (or was for some of you) then things make sense, because when little Meadow June says "Banana" you aren't the only one who hears it. You can turn to someone, say "Wasn't that precious?" And Sara, she says, "Oh my God, yes! Get the phone out. Record her saying it! You got to!" And she's right. You do. And it makes a difference, her holding your arm while she suggests it. It makes a difference that she even suggests it, because you, you wouldn't have thought to record it. It's just not something you do – take pictures, record things, say 'Grace' before eating. But Sara, she does all of that, and you love doing it too – for her, around her, all for her because it's better that way.

That's who Sara is. She's the type of girl you never knew about, that television doesn't acknowledge the existence of. Her friends, they're smart like her. They're educated in things like poverty, poetry, justice, anthropology, music, sociology. Sara, sure, she's beautiful, curls bouncing around her smooth face, but she's started a club called the Feministas and teaches you the word 'feminism' isn't an insult. That's something. And she loves that you write, adores that you adopted a daughter. She even thinks you need to stop only writing into these newsletters, that you need to do even more with your writing because she believes you can, and you think so too as long as you get to do whatever it is you're going to do in life with her, then by God you believe it too. She pushes you with her soft, firm hands, holds you as hard as you hold her back. She's your best friend and you love her, if you're like me.

> *With all my heart & more,*
> *Sam R. Rulik*

There's one more club I haven't tried, and I'm not sure I want to or can or if I should or if so many things, but in the end, it's Poppy who convinces me. Little Meadow June sits bouncing on his knee, distracting Sara who plays with her, making funny faces.

Poppy turns his attention to me, who I was, am, can be. The me before I got to where I am now, part of something. The me alone in the wilderness of my own home eating chocolate between the trees. "Sam," he says, "give it a try. You know you want to."

Dear Parents of the Month Club Children,

It's been a crazy few months for me. I've learned a lot from a lot of people, and I can't say that any one month taught me more than any other or that I am who I am today because of any of them. It's hard to say, if you're me, just what it means to have these people in your life. There were arguments, loving holidays filled with too much of each other, moments where I cried, worried, and understood myself better than ever before. In fact, there were so many things that it's not quite possible to explain them, not worth it, because, in the end, my words, this letter, won't do justice to the importance of parents.

I am thankful there are clubs out there like this one to show my family – to show me – how to learn and love. Let me say that this club, like so many others, has an attribute that shouldn't go ignored. These clubs, these wonderful pieces of life sent to you each month, you can end them at any time – as easy as life can – and as easy as you can begin them. Join in. Be a part of something. My parents taught me that. All of them.

Love,
Sam R. Rulik

PREVIOUS PUBLICATIONS

Some of these stories first appeared in slightly different form in the following magazines:

"A Literary God (in Love)" originally published in *Story Shack Magazine*

"A New Religion for Fatherless Sons" originally published in *Litro*

"After-School Special" originally published in *Nib Magazine*

"Beer of the Month" originally published in *Fiction Attic Press*

"Bloodhounds" originally published in *Extract(s)*

"Casting" originally published in *Five Quarterly*

"Cavemen Until Blue" originally published in *Atticus Review*

"Even Toy Swords" originally published in *Fiction Southeast*

"Future Perfect" originally published in *Sundog Lit*

"Going to Kill a Buffalo" originally published in *Intellectual Refuge*

"Heavy Shoes" originally published in *Bartleby Snopes*

"Her Heart a Thundering Steed" originally published in *Menacing Hedge*

"I Think I'm Going to Make It" originally published in *Communion*

"In Your Father's Backyard" originally published in *Literary Orphans*

"Jim E. Wilson Forgets You" originally published in *Bohemia*

"Life Where You Want It" originally published in *Agave Magazine*

"My Son" originally published in *Flash Fiction Online*

"Pieces of My Junkyard Father" originally published in *Superstition Review*

"Realism in Smiles" originally published in *Pure Coincidence Magazine*

"Seeds of Doubt" originally published in *Gravel*

"She Loves Me Like a Tape Recorder" originally published in *WhiskeyPaper*

"So Bright We Quit Our Shadows" originally published in *Cease, Cows*

"So My Mother, She Lives in the Clouds" originally published in *Psychopomp Magazine*

"Talk of Fire" originally published in *Cease, Cows!*

"That's What You Tell Your Friends" originally published in *CheapPop*

"The Greater Migration" originally published in *Mad Scientist Journal*

"The Last Meal of Mr. Clearwater" originally published in *Litro*

"The Worst Thing About Hell is You Have to Climb Down to It" originally published in *Hypertrophic Literary*

"This Kid's Lightning" originally published in *Sundog Lit*

"Well, This is Change" originally published in *Darkmatter Journal*

"What I Learned Beneath Your Shirt" originally published in *First Stop Fiction*

"When You Die" originally published in *Penduline Press*

"When You're Dead" originally published in *Penduline Press*

"Why the Wolves Take the Calves First" originally published in *Pea River Journal*

"Your Uncle Scott is a Lake Monster" originally published in *Wyvern Lit*

ACKNOWLEDGEMENTS

Many of my stories would have never seen the light of day if it were not for Matthew Kabik, Zachary Woodard, Daniel Difranco, Paul Elwork, and Joshua Isard. The value of a good writing group and a picky professor will never plummet. They are good friends and even better writers who I owe tremendously.

A great many thanks goes to the Arcadia MFA and to the Indie lit community that supports literature in the kindest of ways both in print and online.

Thank you to my family – all of you – who offered your support in so many ways, especially my children. You inspire me.

Thank you to Anna who showed me I could.

And a tremendous thank you to Hypertrophic. None of these stories would have come together in the way that they have if it weren't for the effort and vision of Lynsey Morandin and Jeremy Bronaugh. Their love for the written word gave this collection a way. Thank you.

CPSIA information can be obtained at www.ICGtesting.com
Printed in the USA
LVOW04s0251091015

457588LV00001B/1/P